WOODLAND CHILDREN

BY

SONYA C. DODD

Copyright © 2017 by Sonya C Dodd

All rights reserved. This book or any portion thereof may not be reproduced or used in any manner whatsoever without the express written permission of the publisher except for the use of brief quotations in a book review.

Other titles available by

Sonya C. Dodd:

Woodland Child

A Whisper in the Wind

Harbour of Dreams

Siren Call

Echo of a Siren

Affirmation of the Sirens

Brass Buttons

Dear Mother

2000 words: A collection of short stories

Black Tuesday

Don't Tell Me You're Sorry

The Root of All Evil

With Hindsight

Who's Real?

No Man is an Island

For further details, please check out my website: sonyacdodd.com

Prologue

Silence descends, suffocating life. Life extinguished lies forgotten, abandoned. Mysteriously moving shadows lurk, ebbing and flowing like a tidal wave of fear.

Watchers wait. Petrified branches link fingers, reaching across the void, weaving a welcoming web of imprisonment.

A putrid stench, masked by the icy claws of winters long gone, hangs in the air, heavy with decay.

No laughter remains, no conversation or scampering feet fill the space. They no longer come here, too scared of this once popular playground.

Children tell tales, talking of ghosts, mothers keep them near, even dogs stand and whine by the gate but turn away and leave. Only the occasional outsider may be seen here now, oblivious to the stories and gossip which have built up, the years increasing the horror and detail, creating their own legend and wall of mystery.

In the spring: snowdrops, celandine and then bluebells carpet the malevolent ground, painting an impression of beauty and nature at peace. Summer fills the branches with green: a symbol of new life and harmony. Autumn brings a fiery plain of reds and oranges masking the vengeful earth. A winter's blanket of snow and ice is the last attempt by the seasons to obliterate the scene of death, cover the horror like a final curtain – no applause, nor ovation for the silent players.

A single spotlight on a silent soul, decayed remains marking the shallow grave. The waiting game is afoot, a new victim sought. Patience reigns in the quiet night air; an opportunity for regeneration lies tantalisingly within sight. A new victim is within reach, to be lured slowly and carefully; a trust to be gained, then thwarted: a life for a life.

Her eyes were closed, yet she saw everything. In the early morning coolness, dew covered spiders' webs were painted across footpaths. Droplets of water hung precariously like tiny mirrors reflecting the awakening world.

Enjoy your laughter, she thought, whilst you can.

The sound of the child's laugh shot through the otherwise eerie atmosphere, cracking the silence into two.

She could hear a pair of them, slightly trickier, but their game of hide-and-seek would help to separate them. It would be possible to take two, however one was a more straight-forward proposition – it would be quicker too, and one was all that was necessary.

It wasn't until the girl was underneath the fallen trunk that she noticed the odour. Hearing the numbers being called out rather too hurriedly had made her panic, looking for a good hiding place in these unfamiliar woods; the broken tree had seemed like a blessing. Now, lying on the leaf-littered soil in the darkness, a stomach churning smell had begun seeping into her nostrils when she'd felt her arm brush against some unseen object. Half-listening to the distant sound of her companion's counting voice, Alison's fingers reached out hesitantly.

Something hard, yet soft too, icy to her touch, but moving. The sound of nearby shuffling made her hold her breath. Feeling as if she was being watched, Alison tried to turn her head.

Despite the darkness, her eyes opened wide at the eyes she could see staring back at her. Wanting to scream but too terrified to find the sound of her voice, Alison lay frozen.

She felt the icy, bony fingers curl around her own small, gloved hand.

"Hello," came the whispered sound of a girl's voice. "My name's Amy, what's yours?"

Chapter 1

It is always darkest just before dawn: the darkness of early morning and of our dreams. Jake woke abruptly: bolt upright, heart pounding and bathed in cold sweat. The dream had been so vivid and real, yet, even now, the detail was beginning to fade.

As he sat up with his back now jammed against the headboard of his bed, Jake reflected on what he could remember: he'd been falling from a great height, the feeling of weightlessness together with the earthy and familiar smell of a forest. As Jake's memory of the dream continued to recede still further, he remembered seeing the shape of a small person, possibly a child, as he was falling, but couldn't recall any specific detail.

Easing himself off his bed, Jake swept his hands through his brown, wavy hair and went to the bathroom to relieve his aching bladder whilst the memory of the dream faded still further. Despite this blurring, he couldn't shake the feeling of unease that the dream had left with him, not unlike an unpleasant odour but somehow, far worse than that. He shivered.

The dreams were beginning to become more regular and much more vivid, he realised. At the start, Jake had merely dismissed them as being a result of the shock of losing Amy. His sister's death had been unexpected and sudden which had devastated Jake and his mother. That had been almost ten years ago now.

During the grieving period, Jake had begun to remember there had been small, almost imperceptible, changes in Amy's behaviour which he had dismissed at the time; but now they seemed to have assumed much greater relevance than he'd given them, back then.

After emptying his bladder, Jake decided he couldn't sleep and he would make himself a good, strong cup of coffee. As he padded out onto the landing, past his mother's bedroom, the sound of her heavy breathing was clearly audible as Jake descended the stairs.

His mother was yet another worry for him. Unable to imagine any parent ever recovering from the loss of a child, he'd always tried to make allowances for her grief.

As a teenager, Jake had found it tough, his mum suddenly announcing, every couple of years, that she was unsettled and they needed to move on, yet again. Her tears, anger and self-pity had, in turn, claimed ownership of their lives: ensnaring them, suffocating his mum until moving house had been the only escape from another cycle of torment.

Initially, it would make a difference. She would become the woman he remembered from his early childhood: contented, loving and almost care-free. Then, the shadows would slowly start to descend once more so that it seemed their roles changed until Jake was the parent, supporting a vulnerable child.

He often found himself wondering how he'd ever managed to turn out as 'normal' as he had. Luckily, he always hooked up with a few friends wherever they went and he'd been a good enough student to leave school, and then college, with respectable grades.

It hadn't been as if Marion hadn't tried to help herself: counselling, anti-depressants and support groups had been available like confetti, then abandoned to the rain-washed pavements, discarded reminders of a once hopeful existence.

He wished he had a magic wand; to be able to sweep away the past heartache for his mum and witness the smile on her face as Amy walked back into their lives, was his sole, futile desire.

Now, whenever he found himself watching his mother pottering in the kitchen, or gazing at the television screen, Jake imagined each of the deeply-etched lines on her face as another scar of her suffering, another rung on her downward spiral.

Perhaps, he could've done things differently. Maybe he should have put his foot down and refused to keep moving, forcing her to face reality and deal with her issues: for once and for all. But her tears were always the final straw, not the tears of frustration or anger she'd unleash if he hesitated when he'd come home and discover her searching the internet for cheap lets in yet another city. It was the quiet sobbing which was audible through her bedroom door in the early hours. The sound of her anguish and loss.

There must have been some effect on himself, Jake realised. After all, he'd had a couple of offers from universities, opportunities to move into his own life and put the past firmly behind him. Yet, here he was. Unable to cope with the idea of abandoning his mum, knowing he couldn't possible build a new future for himself whilst she fell apart on her own; Jake had decided to take a year out. Telling his mum, he wanted a chance to earn some money and time to consider what direction he wanted his career to move in, she'd accepted his excuses without question. Jake wasn't even sure she'd realised he was saying the words he believed she would want to hear, just to appease his sense of guilt.

Rinsing his mug and leaving it by the sink, Jake made his mum a tea and carried it carefully upstairs. Out of habit, he knocked gently on the door but pushed it open immediately. As usual, the bedding was in disarray, an indication of his mum's restless night. The other being her gentle snoring now, just as he, and the rest of humankind, on this side of the equator, was getting up to start their day. It was a habit he couldn't break: the tea would go cold on her bedside table and when he got home from work, Jake would carry the full mug, back downstairs to the kitchen. It was foolish, he knew, but he wanted to show his mum he had been thinking about her before he'd gone off to start his day.

He showered and dressed efficiently, glancing briefly at his reflection in the mirror, carefully arranging his hair in a way that made it look tousled, in an attractive manner, as it reached almost to his shoulders and then he adjusted the collar of his shirt, opened casually at the neck. Satisfied with the result, Jake pulled his shoulders back sharply, gave himself a small smile and ran down the stairs, two at a time, hurrying to catch his bus.

Being a waiter wasn't his long-term plan. However, the hours were flexible, the people he worked with were a good bunch and money from tips helped to supplement his income.

Jake dreamt of travelling one day, although that would have to wait until he was confident his mum could cope without him and Jake wasn't optimistic of that happening any time soon.

Sometimes Jake thought his mum assumed she was the only person who still missed Amy. Her sudden death had rocked the whole village they'd been living in at the time and as a, then, ten-year-old boy, Jake hadn't really understood what had happened. Whilst his mum had been busy dealing with everyone and everything, he had been handed from one friend's parent to another, apparently being protected from unnecessary angst and leading as normal a life as was possible under the circumstances.

Amy had been older than him, they'd not been overly close, mainly due to the age gap, but her death had left a gaping hole in their lives which had never been closed. Marion never talked about Amy, there were no photographs of his sister in their home, not on display anyway. It made sense, his mum had been bereft, she had never been able to deal with Amy's death, and didn't need constant reminders that there had once been three of them.

His dad had walked out on them whilst he was still a baby, so Jake had no memory of him. Being determined to make a success of raising her children alone, without the support of a man, had made his mum fiercely independent and determined. Somehow, Amy's death had seemed to take that away. The transformation had been immediate and long-lasting. It was probably the thing Jake found hardest to deal with. It was as if she'd forgotten she had another child. Seemingly, giving up on parenthood as a failed experiment, Jake had brought himself up, as well as keeping his mum moving slowly forward through life. He didn't want her thanks; more than anything, Jake just wanted his mum back.

Amy had been a loner. Jake had known better than trying to get his big sister to play with him. She was either ensconced in her bedroom, the door firmly shut against the outside world, or, she was out walking the dog.

She'd spent more time with Patch than with either Jake or their mum. Amy knew everything about plants and animals and loved being in the woods or on the hills surrounding their home. Jake used to wonder whether she'd been an animal in a previous life, being much happier when she was wandering the countryside, rather than stuck indoors. Now, Jake liked to think of Amy as a bird – free to fly wherever she chose.

That had been the one good thing about moving away from his childhood home and leaving their friends behind: in other places, they had anonymity. No longer seen as the grieving brother, Jake had found relief in shaking off the constant sympathy and whispering behind his back. It was tough starting afresh: making new friends, getting used to new schools and new teachers. However, Jake had a secret: one friend who did know all about his past and what had happened to his sister.

Funnily enough, Martha had joined Jake's school almost immediately after Amy's death. He had become good friends with her very quickly, despite his mum's inexplicable dislike of the girl. Through all the paraphernalia which had gone on after Amy's disappearance, Martha had been a constant in Jake's life. She'd been there when his mother hadn't; Martha had listened to him and offered words of comfort, been more sympathetic than his male counterparts.

When his mum had said they were moving away, the first thought Jake had was: 'How would he cope without Martha?' So, secretly, they had kept in touch; initially written notes had been posted and intercepted. Then, as they'd got older, the easy availability of the internet and social media had helped to maintain their covert friendship with much greater simplicity.

Without Martha, Jake was convinced he would have gone quite mad. The responsibility of looking after his mum was immense for someone so young, and having a friend he could pour out his feelings with honesty to, helped Jake to keep everything in perspective.

It had been a shame they'd never managed to meet up in the intervening years. Even when Jake had suggested it, for a rare weekend when his mother was in better spirits, Martha had maintained she was unable to leave home to see him. Jake couldn't understand her reluctance to have a break from the familiar setting of Bradfield, yet he could hardly admonish her, when he remained by his mother's side so resolutely.

Sometimes, they'd go weeks, or even months, without exchanging an email or text, but it was always comfortable and easy when the familiar name re-appeared in his inbox; Jake would click the button with a smile on his face and their conversation would continue as if there'd been no break.

Suddenly today, Jake found himself thinking about Martha. He'd not heard from her for a while, he realised. He'd been serving a couple of young women at a table and one of them had really reminded Jake of Martha, with her dark hair and brown eyes. It had been difficult not to be caught staring at her, after he'd initially thought it was Martha paying him a surprise visit.

Unable to shake off his disappointment, Jake had decided he would email her when he got home and try, once again, to set up a reunion.

Although Jake enjoyed his job, physically it was demanding: standing all day, maintaining a constant smile for the customers and carrying the plates and trays of glasses backwards and forwards between the kitchen and dining room.

Considering himself fortunate to have landed a waiting job in a hotel, just after moving once again, Jake's employers had been impressed with his references, if not a little surprised by how many places he'd managed to work in for someone of his age. Jake tried to avoid telling anyone about Amy; she lived in his heart and inside his head, but he wasn't after anyone's sympathy and certainly didn't want to use her death as a reason to get a job.

Occasionally, if his mum was in a really bad way, Jake was forced to explain why he needed so much time off; usually his boss was pretty accommodating; it was why he worked hard, to keep in their good books in case he needed to ask any favours in the future.

Working in a hotel, Jake enjoyed the variety he sometimes got from working in such a place. If required, he could cover in the kitchen, serve in the bar, as well as numerous other jobs which seemed in never-ending supply. The fact they were constantly busy suited Jake; he never had a chance to get bored. Of course, on the down-side, it meant he was exhausted by the end of a shift, which could last up to ten hours on some occasions.

"You still here?"

Jake looked up from the glass he was meticulously cleaning with a cloth. He grinned at the familiar sound of the head chef's voice. Pasquale was Italian; sometimes he spoke so quickly as he barked out orders that Jake found it difficult following what he was saying. However, he was a fair person to work for and Jake was always pleased when he got to work in the kitchen: the work was demanding but there was a great sense of team-work. The small Italian could be fierce, but he also ran an efficient kitchen, was an amazing cook and knew how to keep a happy crew of workers. He and Jake had spent many an evening, after everything had been done and was ready for the new onslaught the following day, cradling a drink and putting the world to rights. It felt good to have someone looking out for him, almost like a father figure.

"How's your mother?" Pasquale asked, coming to a standstill by Jake and picking up one of the glasses, he held it up, slowly turning it in the light.

"Oh, you know," Jake replied vaguely. He'd spoken to Pasquale from time to time about his home life; it helped ease the burden a bit, just being able to voice his concerns and he knew Pasquale was trustworthy.

"Not too good," he replied knowingly. It was evident Jake wasn't in the mood for a chat so Pasquale told him not to work too much longer and left him to it.

Yawning and stretching his tired limbs, Jake threw down his cloth and stared at the surface filled with, now, sparkling glasses. Light danced off the gleaming crystal, mesmerising his weary eyes. Thinking only of his welcoming bed and soft duvet waiting to embrace him, Jake flicked the light off and headed for the bus station.

It looked as if every light was on in the house as Jake slipped his key into the front door. Feeling exhausted, he'd hoped his mum might already be in bed when he got home so he could shower off the smells of the kitchen and fall into bed as quickly as possible.

When he stepped into the hall and closed the door behind him, it was as if his mum had been watching and waiting for him. Immediately, she appeared in the sitting room doorway and Jake could see from her expression, she wasn't happy.

"Why didn't you tell me?" Marion demanded.

"Hi Mum, lovely to see you too. How was your day? Mine? Exhausting but thanks for asking." Jake sang his spiel, hoping to ease the tension leeching from his mother.

"Jacob Brooks," she scolded. "I'm being serious."

"Yes, I can see that," Jake replied, cringing at his mother's use of 'Jacob.' "Can we, at least, sit down before you tell me what the problem is?" he put his hand on his mum's shoulder and gently eased past her so he could collapse onto the sofa. Jake had the impression his mum's tirade could last some time, listening to the tone of her voice. At least she was alert which was a good sign.

As Jake sank onto the sofa, aware his mum was perched on the arm of a chair, arms crossed and watching him, it was only when he glanced down at the coffee table in front of him that Jake saw his laptop sitting open.

"What's that doing there?" he demanded, pulling himself forward. "You've been in my room!"

If Jake had expected to find his mum looking guilty, he was disappointed.

"It's just as well I did go in there," Marion declared, showing no sign of remorse. "Why didn't you tell me you had kept in touch with *her*?"

"What?" Jake cried, frowning.

"Don't play innocent with me, young man. You know perfectly well I'm talking about Martha."

Jake's head felt like it had become full of cotton wool. He moved the mouse on his laptop and the screen lit up, revealing the inbox to his emails. "You've been going through my private stuff?"

Jake shook his head. He was dumb-founded. "What d'you think you're doing?"

"What about *her*? What's she doing emailing you?" Marion countered, ignoring her son's questions.

"Who are you going on about?" Jake asked, confused by his mum's attitude and hurt by the way she'd invaded his privacy without any apparent hesitation.

"Martha!" Marion screeched.

Jake looked incredulously at his mum. "Is that what this is all about?" he asked quietly. "You're snooping through my stuff and getting yourself in a state because I kept in touch with someone I went to primary school with – and only for a few weeks at that!"

"Why, Jake, why?"

He looked at her as she began sobbing into her hands. His anger at his mum's intrusion was replaced with confusion. Why was she letting herself get so worked up over a few emails exchanged with an old friend? It didn't make any sense; her state was all out of proportion with his apparent crime.

Dragging himself off the sofa, Jake sat in the armchair and pulled his mum down beside him, his arm around her shoulder as he waited for her crying to subside.

At length, as she became quieter, Jake decided to risk the question, burning on his lips: "What's your problem with Martha? You never liked her, did you?"

Marion blew her nose and then gazed down at the crumpled tissue, lying in her hands. "She was evil, Jake; you must have sensed it," she muttered quietly as though the wind had suddenly been knocked out of her sails.

Jake took his arm from behind her back and leaned forward to face her. "She was a young girl! She'd had a rough start in life; maybe she was a bit odd, in the things she said or how she behaved, but Martha was harmless. She was a good friend to me after Amy …" Leaving his sentence unfinished, Jake had to look away from the sheer torment etched in his mum's face. Filled with confusion, Jake felt as though they were speaking two separate languages, neither of them being able to understand the other. Surely, as mother and son, they should have a strong sense of connection.

"I'm sorry, Mum, if I've upset you somehow," Jake admitted. "But I've never understood why you had a problem with Martha. That's why I kept it a secret from you that we used to write to each other, I knew you wouldn't approve. Then, over time, I just stopped thinking about it. You've never bothered about who I chose as my friends before and I can't see why Martha should be any different."

Jake's head ached. He was shattered after a long day at work. All he'd hoped for was a quiet, early night when he came home; he didn't need an argument with his mum about something this irrational. "Are you still on the sleeping tablets?" he asked innocently.

"What's that got to do with anything?" Marion suddenly yelled, standing up and turning to face him. "You had no right keeping that from me, no doubt laughing about what happened with that scheming little bitch."

"Whoa," Jake held his hands up and stood to face his mother, ignoring the fact he towered over her by nearly a foot. "We need to back-pedal here a bit. What is your problem with Martha?"

Marion paused, apparently weighing up how to respond. Then, appearing to throw caution to the wind, she exclaimed: "That bitch killed your sister." She was panting heavily and lowered herself back onto the chair as if exhausted.

Jake stared at his mother, her words ringing in his ears. Slowly, he shook his head. "I don't know where you got such a ridiculous idea from, but you know that's not true. It's absurd," he replied quietly.

"Can't you recall how she turned up? Coincidently, just after Amy died?" Marion asked.

Jake shook his head again. "So? That makes a ten-year-old kid a killer, does it?" Jake cringed at the way his voice was rising. How, on earth, had his mum come up with such a stupid idea? Had she been weaving this fabrication inside her head all these years?

"You were young, Jake; you didn't really understand what was going on," Marion replied.

"No," Jake interrupted her. "I knew my sister was dead! But, apart from that, you shut me out of everything else and passed me from one person to another whilst you were fully aware of everything that happened; and I can assure you, none of it had anything to do with Martha. Thank God for Martha!" Jake exclaimed, throwing up his arms in frustration, now they'd opened up all the old wounds. "I'm glad she did arrive when she did because she was the only person who bothered asking me how I felt, and listened to my side."

Marion simply stared at Jake, taken aback by his uncharacteristic outburst. His head was bent as his shoulders shook; she'd never seen him like this and it frightened her. Slowly, Marion reached out and took his hand in hers. His fingers hung loosely, despite the contact.

"I'm sorry, Jake," Marion whispered. "Please sit down so we can talk about this."

Jake glanced across at his mother's upturned face. "I've got nothing to say," he told her. "Martha's my friend. I don't care whether you like her or not, it doesn't matter. But I'm not going to listen to your lies about her, and I'm certainly not going to stop talking to her just because of some fanciful stories swimming round in your head. Now, I'm shattered, it's been a long day and I'm going to bed."

Jake scooped up his laptop and left his mum looking after him as he disappeared upstairs to bed. He had no idea how long she continued to sit downstairs; as soon as his head hit the pillow, sleep enveloped him.

Chapter 2

The unfamiliar sound of someone in the kitchen woke Jake the next morning. He'd spent years waking to his radio alarm or a silent home, so the noise of clanking pots and pans, drawers opening and closing, was an alien concept. Clearly, his ears had alerted his brain to the possibility of a break-in; but as he rubbed his eyes and the grey light of morning poured into his consciousness, Jake relaxed. Glancing at his alarm clock, he noted it was nearly seven. Mentally, Jake checked his work rota and recalled he was doing lunches and dinner today so he didn't need to be in until late morning. Groaning slightly, he tucked his hand under his pillow and settled onto his side, eyes closing again.

The peace was momentary; his mother's voice carried upstairs: "Jake! Breakfast's ready."

Jake's eyes shot open. Glancing at the clock again, he saw the time had only moved on by one minute; he couldn't have been dreaming. His mum had prepared breakfast? Jake couldn't remember a time when his mum had made his breakfast, or even been up before he was already downstairs and getting ready for the day ahead. Something was really wrong, he decided, as he threw back his duvet and slid out of bed; this needed investigation. If nothing else, she'd certainly piqued his curiosity.

Creeping into the kitchen, Jake stared at the unfamiliar sight of his mum at the cooker, spatula in hand as she turned and smiled at his entrance. She even laughed at the expression she saw on his face.

"Come on, you," she giggled. "Sit yourself down, your coffee's on the table: strong, just as you like it."

Jake wandered to the table and sank onto a chair like a zombie. The table was laid for one with knife and fork, a glass of orange juice and mug of coffee, both poured. Even the cruet set and brown sauce, waited expectantly for his arrival. Wearing only a T-shirt and his boxer shorts, Jake shivered, unsure whether it was the cold, or shock, which made him do so.

Almost immediately, Marion placed a plate of bacon and fried egg in front of him. Okay, Jake thought, the egg needed a little less time: the yolk was hard and it had begun to crisp around the edges, the bacon looked adequately cooked. He poked it cautiously with his knife.

"It's okay," Marion said, laughing. "I can remember how to cook; I used to do it all the time when we lived in Bradfield."

"You mean, when Amy was alive," Jake prompted sulkily. His memory of their conversation the night before was returning. There was a lot they still had to say to each other, but he wasn't sure he was ready for that at this time of the morning, especially when he was reeling from the shock of his mother cooking him breakfast.

Marion, cradling her own mug of tea, sat down facing him and Jake, wishing to show some gratitude for her efforts, began eating obediently.

It felt strange, having her watching him. He'd been so used to having the house to himself first thing each day, for so long, that Jake couldn't help but feel violated by this interruption to the routine he'd built quite happily for himself.

Certainly, it was promising to see his mum make such an effort, uncharacteristic maybe, but encouraging, nonetheless. He didn't want to knock her fragile improvement, but he still wanted to understand what her problem was with Martha. There was no way he was going to give up his friendship with his childhood friend, yet, now they'd started the conversation, it would have to be finished.

Her constant smiling as he put each mouthful between his lips was disconcerting. It was great to see his mother this animated, even if it had been caused by her anger, anything was better than the quiet indifference she'd shown for so long in every aspect of their lives.

Her hands never settled, Jake noticed. Either she was fiddling with the mug, or straightening an invisible table cloth. As far as he knew, his mum had never been a smoker but she was behaving like an ex-smoker at the moment.

"So, what's this in aid of?" Jake asked, laying his cutlery down and swapping his empty plate for his coffee. "It's not my birthday, or Christmas."

Marion watched him earnestly. "I'm sorry, Jake; I've been a crap mum, I know. It's been tough; I wish I could've been stronger than I have, but it all just fell apart." Her voice cracked slightly and she stopped speaking.

Jake could see the effect of the effort she'd taken, not only in getting out of bed and making him breakfast, but also in talking to him like this; they hadn't had a proper conversation for years, he realised.

Raising her mug to her mouth, to give herself time to pull herself together again, Marion knew her hands were shaking. It was all she could do to stop the tea splashing out onto the table. Now, looking at her son, all grown up and seemingly so wise, it was tough realising how much she had missed out on in his life.

The truth had hit her hard the night before. Never having had the chance to watch Amy turn from a girl into a woman, Marion realised with a heavy heart, her son had transformed from a boy into a man without her witnessing it. Her eyes had been closed, just as her heart had remained frozen, an instinct against being burdened with any further, unnecessary pain after her daughter's death.

Now, feeling the unfamiliar sensation of her own thawing, Marion looked at Jake with pride. As much as he might have had to shoulder his own upbringing and look after his crazy mother, into the bargain, she knew she'd let him down terribly. There were no excuses, and she held up her hand when he tried to defend her behaviour. Marion knew she didn't deserve Jake. He'd always been a good boy; he'd been quite entitled to go off the rails, why he didn't, she had no idea. Looking at the man sitting before her, Marion cringed at the fact of how little she really knew him. Just knowing he'd kept up his friendship with Martha though, when Marion had assumed all thoughts of her had been left buried in the village where they'd laid Amy's body to rest, had terrified her.

For most of the night, Marion had remained awake as her mind slowly peeled back the memories of that appalling period of their lives. Foolishly, she'd thought she was strong enough to get over their loss and could continue to be a mum and a dad for Jake; clearly, she'd managed to be neither.

Now, Marion knew she had to find some strength from somewhere deep inside her if she wasn't going to risk losing Jake. The girl he seemed to cherish so inexplicably, was his sister's killer. Martha had admitted as much to Marion when she'd faced her, shortly after Amy's death. Yet, Marion had been unable to share their conversation with anyone and Martha had been fully aware of that. After all, who would have believed Amy had been murdered by a ghost who wanted their own life back in exchange for her daughter's? Martha already had her claws firmly embedded in Jake's friendship and Marion didn't dare risk losing Jake to social services if she'd started accusing a small girl of killing her own daughter, for no apparent reason.

She'd tried to block Martha out and carry on their lives in the same village, but the pressure inside her was unrelenting. Not only was Martha happy to parade herself in the school playground, arm in arm with Jake, there were also the painful reminders everywhere of Amy. Her dog, Patch, had seemingly pined away his existence after her death and not lived much longer. Every time she heard a bird singing, or noticed a new flower in their garden coming into blossom, it was like a stab through her heart as Amy's face seemed to loom into her vision.

Maybe it had been daft to imagine the pain could diminish, simply by leaving the village, but she'd had to try something or risk going completely crazy and losing custody of Jake anyway.

"I know it's been hard for you," Jake was saying. "But I think of her every single day too."

Marion hung her head, gazing unseeingly at her lap. "I'm sorry, Jake," she repeated. "I never paused to think about your grief. I was too wrapped up in my own emotions to consider you'd lost your sister. I suppose, you just seemed to be carry on as you always had, it didn't occur to me you might be doing it for my benefit, rather than because you could."

"I don't want you to feel bad, Mum," Jake sighed. "It's done; I survived and now here we are."

Marion laughed. "How do you always manage to sound like the adult?"

"I am an adult now," he replied quickly. "You see?" he asked, pointing towards his own body. "I'm all grown up, Mum."

Shaking her head, Marion couldn't keep the smile from her lips. It didn't bear thinking about: where she might have ended up without this lovely, strapping lad by her side throughout the years. Her gratitude now felt like an empty offering but it was all she had to give him.

Jake drained the contents of his mug and put it down on the table. "I've got to go and grab a shower before work," he told her, standing up and planting a kiss on her head. "Thanks for breakfast," he added.

"Hang on, Jake," Marion cried, grabbing his hand before he could disappear. "We need to talk about Martha."

Jake rolled his eyes and paused. "I'm not giving up my friendship with her, whatever you say."

"Jake," Marion sighed, "she's bad news. I lost Amy, please, I can't lose you as well."

Jake shook his head. "I'm sorry, Mum, I know you don't like her; I don't need you to like her. But I'm not giving her up; she's important to me."

Marion felt Jake pull his hand slowly from her grasp. As he walked towards the door, she turned in her chair to face him. "Please, Jake, I'm begging you."

Jake paused. Then, he walked back to the table. "This is ridiculous. Stop it now; either tell me why you don't like Martha, or just let it go and accept she's my friend."

"I've told you, Jake, that girl murdered your sister." Marion watched an array of emotions sweep across her son's face.

"Why are you doing this? Why now? I've been friends with Martha for a decade; I'm still here. Nothing's going to happen to me, certainly not at the hands of Martha. You know, you need to let Amy go, Mum. This has gone on long enough, screwing you up inside. Martha's been a constant in my life. I know this will sound hurtful, I don't mean it to be, but she's been there for me when you haven't."

Inside, Jake cringed as he heard himself speaking his final words. He watched as the colour drained from his mum's face.

"She's won," Marion muttered almost inaudibly. "You've done exactly what she wanted," she continued more firmly.

Frowning, Jake held out his hands towards her in disbelief. "What have I done? Been a good friend? Supported you by being a good son?"

"No, Jake," Marion screamed at him. "You've been the perfect son and a pawn in her game. Look at us! We're tearing each other apart over her, exactly what she'd want."

"No!" Jake exclaimed, holding a raised finger at his mum's face. "You're the only one here tearing us apart. Martha's not here, she never has been. It's all up here," he declared as he tapped the side of her head with his finger. Before she could respond, Jake turned heel and ran up the stairs, slamming the bathroom door behind him.

Eventually, when Jake went downstairs to leave for work, he found his mum standing at the bottom of the stairs, holding his jacket out towards him like a peace offering.

Her face was streaked with tears and Jake felt a lump in his throat as he accepted the proffered jacket. "Thanks," he mumbled.

"I don't want us to fight," Marion told him as he walked straight past her and opened the front door.

For a moment, he hesitated, door knob in his hand. But, without turning to look at her, he left the house without a backward glance.

The bus journey and lunch shift passed by in a haze. Jake tried to force the memory of his argument with his mum out of his head after he messed up one order; yet snippets crept relentlessly into his mind.

By the time he took a break and sat down with a bowl of pasta for his own lunch, Jake was exhausted. His head ached and he wanted nothing more than to climb into bed and fall into a dreamless sleep. Glancing at his watch though, he noted there was another six hours before he could think about heading home again.

Stabbing at his pasta as if it had caused him some harm, Jake didn't notice Pasquale approaching, until he slid onto the bench next to him.

Jake glanced up and nodded, as he chewed a mouthful of food; and noticed his friend's plate piled with salad and chips, smothered in a sweet chilli sauce. "That looks revolting," he commented, still chewing.

"That's alright," Pasquale chuckled, "I don't need you to eat it for me." He shovelled a forkful of chips into his mouth as if to prove the point.

Jake returned his attention, half-heartedly, to his own lunch. He became aware of Pasquale watching him and he pulled himself more upright to try and look like he was grateful for his food.

"What's up with you then?" Pasquale asked at length.

Jake shrugged. "Nothin'," he sighed.

"Ah, c'mon," he replied, nudging Jake's arm with his elbow. "I've known you long enough now to know when you're not happy."

Looking at his companion, Jake smiled as best he could. "It's just Mum," he mumbled.

"Your mother? Is she unwell?"

Jake smiled at the genuine concern in his friend's face. "No," he began, "She's fine, pretty good for her actually. This morning, she was out of bed and even made me breakfast; I must have been ten the last time that happened."

"What you worried about then!" Pasquale exclaimed, nudging Jake again, enthusiastically.

"She's just got some weird ideas. She doesn't like one of my friends, doesn't want me to have anything to do with her."

"Ah," Pasquale sighed, knowingly. "It is a girl! Mothers find it difficult to accept their little boys will have girlfriends." His heavy Italian accent lilted as he mentioned girls.

Jake gave a chuckle. If only it was that simple, he thought. "No, it's not like that. Martha's an old school friend. I haven't seen her for years but we kept in touch," he explained.

Pasquale frowned. "What's her problem then? Why doesn't your mother like this girl?"

Jake shook his head, searching his mind for a way to put the problem into words which might make sense. The whole thing was stupid though. His mum had been letting this thing with Martha build inside her for years. He wondered, again, what had made her go into his room and look at his laptop; Jake made a mental note to quiz her later.

"It's a long story," Jake replied. "Let's just say, Mum never liked her and didn't like it when she found out I'd kept in touch with Martha all these years."

"Ah," Pasquale sighed, rubbing his chin thoughtfully. He seemed to turn his attention back to his lunch and Jake assumed the discussion was closed.

When his plate was empty, as he laid his knife and fork together, Pasquale gave Jake a sidelong glance. "You gonna see this girl?"

For a moment, Jake was confused. Then he recalled what they'd been talking about and shook his head. "I doubt it."

"Why not? You like her?" Pasquale was now standing but paused, his plate in his hand, whilst he looked at Jake.

Jake shrugged. "Yes, I like her," he admitted. "Don't s'pose I'll see her though." He picked up his own bowl and slid out of his seat.

"Why not? You need to sort this out, Jake. If your mother doesn't like this girl but she is important to you, why don't you go and see her? See if she is willing to visit your mother so you don't have to feel like the pig in the centre."

"Piggy in the middle," Jake corrected. "I don't know. It would be nice to see her, but it would be strange, after all these years."

"Well, it's up to you, my boy, but if I was you, I know that's what I would do. Take some holiday; you look like you need it." Pasquale gave Jake a brief smile and then disappeared into the kitchen.

Jake stood still, thinking. It was a pleasant idea; if Martha wouldn't come to him, maybe he could surprise her and visit there instead. It would be weird to go back, and he wasn't sure how he would feel about it, but there could only be one way of finding out. It had never been an option before, with his mum being so up and down. But if she remained on top of things as she was at the moment, Pasquale was right, why shouldn't he take a break?

When Jake got home that night, the house was dark and silent. His mum had left the outside light on for him, but apart from that there was no sign of life. Jake was glad. He was shattered and didn't fancy the idea of an argument. He slipped off his jacket and shoes and crept upstairs to his room.

Apart from his bed being made, everything looked as he'd left it. Dropping onto his bed, Jake laid back and stared at the ceiling. He'd not had chance to think about Pasquale's suggestion since lunch; the restaurant had been busy and a couple of staff had called in sick so it had been a case of: all hands-on deck. The stress of the day seemed to fall off him. Closing his eyes, Jake let his mind wander back to Low Bradfield.

He hadn't wanted to move away, but of course, being only ten years old at the time, Jake wasn't given a say in the matter. They were moving and that was that.

At first it had been like a holiday. It was summer and they'd stayed with his mum's sister and her family so he'd had a laugh and there was always plenty of company. It was a world away from the small village they'd left behind. Their cottage had been the only home Jake had known and he'd had a great bunch of friends. Being part of a small community, there had been a lot of freedom, with everyone watching out for each other. It was probably the last time Jake had enjoyed that kind of independence.

Everything changed when they moved into their own place. With just him and his mum, the walls seemed to close in on their lives. Even when he went off to school each day, he was under strict orders to come straight home. On the odd occasion, he'd thrown caution to the wind and dared to stay out for a game of football with his mates, the terror his mum had experienced as she described how worried she'd been when he'd not come home at his usual time, made those times a rarity.

It seemed strange to Jake. His mum could appear so out of it, totally oblivious to anything going on around them, that he was always surprised she even noticed he was late home. In a way, he liked it. Her concern, whilst clearly painful for her, showed that she was aware of his presence and he was important to her.

Jake realised, he must have known his mum wouldn't approve of his continued friendship with Martha, otherwise he wouldn't have been so secretive about their exchange of letters. He seemed to recall it was Martha who had originally suggested they be secret pen pals. She was aware his mum didn't really like her, but it never bothered her. In fact, now he came to think of it, Martha had found it funny, for some reason known only to her. However, she'd insisted he said nothing to his mum and had given him a supply of paper and envelopes to ensure he kept his promise to write. He'd even found an initial sheet of stamps for his letters, in amongst his gift.

Martha had definitely been the one who was instrumental in continuing their friendship, especially at first. Whenever his letters were too tardy in arriving, he'd always get a curt note from her, admonishing him, accusing him of not caring about her any longer and suggesting he had too many new friends to bother about his old ones. Of course, her plan had worked; Jake was always then catapulted into action and would sit pouring over the empty page until it was filled with his scruffy scrawl and sealed in an envelope ready for posting.

Martha. Jake pictured her in his head. She'd stood out. Not only was she the new girl, she knew what she wanted and went to any length to get it. Boys didn't scare her, and she was, somehow, above the other girls. Yes, she was pretty: long, dark hair and brown eyes which contrasted with her pale complexion. She might have been small, but she would stand up to anyone who dared cross her. Jake recalled, he'd been flattered when she'd seemed to pick him out to be her closest friend. He hadn't minded, he'd always made friends easily and assumed Martha had picked this up, finding him approachable.

She'd been very curious to come to his home, Jake remembered. He'd been really scared his mum would explode the day she found Martha in Amy's bedroom. It had been a genuine mistake; she'd not known where the bathroom was but his mum hadn't bought it as an excuse. Amy's room had been like a shrine and Martha had trodden on the sacrality of the place.

Her 'goodbye' kiss had thrown Jake. He'd been expecting a peck on the cheek. Embarrassed by the fuss she was making about it, in the playground, with all his mates watching too, he recalled Martha had placed both hands on his shoulders and pulled him towards her possessively. Her lips had stuck to his like glue and he'd just stood there cringing with awkwardness, listening to his friends' laughter surrounding them until she'd finally released him and he'd been able to escape.

Of course, it had been the first thing she'd mentioned in her initial letter to him. He'd not kept any of them, although he could imagine her having a secret stash of his correspondence. He'd been too scared of his mum's reaction if she'd found any of them; as it turned out, it was just as well he'd thrown them all away.

Jake had told her he'd been too shy, in front of their classmates, to kiss her back but promised, as she'd made him, that it had been the best kiss he'd ever had. Of course, he didn't bother mentioning it was the first kiss he'd had, apart from those from his mum and other family members.

Certainly, Martha could be very earnest, frightening sometimes, but she'd been the one he'd poured out his concerns to, about his mum, and described the ups and downs of his developing, young life.

Jake wondered what had made his mum say the things she had about Martha, especially accusing her of being his sister's killer. Everyone knew Amy had fallen from the top of the hill; it had been an accident, it was what he'd read on the coroner's report.

She must have been very scared and lonely as she'd dragged herself into the woods. It was painful, even now, to think of his sister alone in her dying moments. She'd always been so happy outside, but it was that place which had taken her from them. Nothing at all to do with Martha.

Maybe it was just the worst thing his mum could think of to say to try and get him to stop being friends with Martha. It was vindictive and if Martha ever found out his mum thought that, Jake was positive she'd be really upset. She'd asked after his mum every time she'd written and often discussed her at length, almost as if his mum was hers too.

Jake felt his annoyance stirring inside him again, remembering his mum's words from the morning. He forced the thoughts from his head; he needed sleep, not anger about something he couldn't do anything about right now.

"Tell me this is a joke," Marion warned, the following morning, when Jake had told her of his plan to visit Low Bradfield.

Jake had experienced mixed emotions when he'd seen his mum was up and about again the next day. It was a relief to see she'd got herself out of bed voluntarily for a second time in a row; yet, Jake also knew she'd put up a fight about him going back.

"It's not a joke; I'm going," he replied bluntly.

"But you can't," Marion declared, pulling back the chair sharply and sitting down to face her son.

"Mum," Jake began, leaning back from his breakfast and looking at her. "I'm twenty. You can't stop me. For goodness sake, I could fly to the other side of the world if I wanted to, but I don't. I'm going back to Bradfield for a few days, and then I'll be home again, before you know it." He picked up his glass and drained the orange juice into his mouth. Swallowing the sour liquid, Jake watched his mum as he then began picking bits of bacon from between his teeth.

"But why, Jake?" she cried. "Of all the places, why there?"

"Why not?" he said, shrugging and inspecting the morsel of bacon, on his finger, he'd managed to retrieve.

"Because it's where your sister died?" Marion suggested. "It's so morbid wanting to go back to that place," she spat.

"You lived there enough years; it can't have been that bad."

"I can't believe you!" Marion cried in exasperation. "Have you listened to yourself? Have you no respect for your sister's memory?"

Jake wiped his finger on his jumper and looked down. "Of course I have. That's part of the reason I want to go back. I was a little kid when we left. I want to see if it's like I remember; I can visit her grave whilst I'm there." He glanced up at his mum. It was clear she was upset; he'd known she would be. But Jake now felt he had to do this, like laying the ghosts of the past to rest.

"Why don't you come with me?" he suggested.

Marion looked askance. "Are you really serious? After everything we went through in that village?"

"You might find it a comfort," Jake risked. "you've spent so long grieving and reliving what happened, perhaps you need to do this too."

Shaking her head, Marion kept her eyes fixed on her son's face. "I suppose this is *her* idea?"

Jake frowned and raised an eyebrow.

"Her! Martha!" Marion exclaimed, her words crammed with disgust.

"You're wrong!" Jake replied, smiling and pushing back his chair, he folded his arms across his chest. "Martha doesn't know anything about it; I thought I would surprise her, yes. But it was actually Pasquale's idea."

Marion had never met Pasquale but she had heard Jake mention him several times. "Well, he needs to keep his ideas to himself," Marion told him. "He wasn't there; I take it he doesn't know what happened."

"Bits of it," Jake confessed. "I thought it was a great idea though, so I'm going. I don't need your permission, I'm not asking for it. I just thought you'd like to know I won't be around for a couple of days."

"What about work?" Marion asked, searching her mind desperately for obstacles.

"They're fine about it. I've worked straight through the summer; suits them if I take some leave now before we get busy again in the lead up to Christmas."

Marion watched as her son's face disappeared behind his mug. She couldn't understand why he was doing this now. Why did he suddenly get the desire to go back to that place after so long? The older, better memories, when Amy had been with them had been obliterated by what had happened. Maybe it was some morbid curiosity which was driving him to do this. Whatever his reason, Marion had a nasty feeling it wasn't about to be easy, for either of them.

Jake put his mug down on the table. "By the way," he began, "Why did you go into my laptop?"

Marion cringed. She wasn't proud of what she'd done. She'd had no idea it would have led to all this. "I saw something on the news; I wanted to look it up on the internet for more information," she explained. "I didn't realise it would be open on your email when I clicked the internet."

"What about your phone? Why couldn't you have used that?"

"Oh Jake," Marion sighed. "You know how small my screen is. If I was going to read through the newspapers, I wanted something I could actually see without straining my eyes."

Jake wriggled in his seat. It made sense, but it still didn't tell him what she'd been so interested in. He asked her.

"It was about a disappearance, if you must know," Marion told him. "Some girl, on holiday in the Peak District, funnily enough, near Bradfield, has gone missing. It just reminded me of Amy and what we went through, I guess," Marion continued.

Marion sat back as her mind flittered to the reports she'd read. There were so many similarities, it had pushed her back into the past when she'd first realised Amy was missing. The fact this girl had disappeared around the same woods where they had found Amy's body had made it even more relevant.

Suddenly, Marion stood up.

"What's wrong?" Jake asked, seeing the look of horror on her face.

"I'd forgotten about the body," Marion whispered.

Jake looked at her, confused. "What body?"

"Can't you remember? Maybe you were too young," she said vaguely. "Amy came home from walking Patch one night. She was in a right state. I remember her coming into the kitchen as pale as a sheet, like she'd seen a ghost. Then she told me she'd found a girl's dead body in the woods. Anyway, she was so frightened, I couldn't help but believe her. We went to the police station and then had to go up into the woods with them so Amy could show them where she'd found the body, you see?"

Jake nodded as vague memories came into his mind.

"Anyway, there was nothing there. I think the poor girl was totally embarrassed by it all, think she took a bit of ribbing about it too. Don't you think it's odd though?"

Jake ground his teeth and shrugged. "If there'd been a body there, maybe. But if Amy just imagined it all then there can't be a coincidence, only that Amy's body was found in the woods. This girl might have gone missing near there, but there's no reason to presume that's where she is, even if she is dead. For all we know they might have found her by now, safe and well."

Marion ignored Jake's comments. She could recall the last time she'd felt like this and her instinct was telling her she was right to be alarmed again. Back then, she'd discovered there had been a body found in those woods, years before they moved there, long before Amy was even alive. And then, through her own investigations, Marion had learnt that body had belonged to the girl who they came to know as Martha. It had been complicated: Martha had died at the hands of her father and then Amy had come along to the site where her body had lain and stirred up her ghost, or some such thing. Her daughter's grim discovery had led to her demise as Martha had pursued Amy to her death, apparently so she could live again.

Marion hadn't even tried to explain any of this to Jake. She was aware how fantastical it sounded, and there was only her word against Martha's. Certainly, there had been no possibility of taking her findings to the police.

Could this disappearance be linked in any way to Martha or Amy's death? Marion pondered. It seemed an even stronger reason for Jake not to go back there, but how could she begin to make him understand?

An uncomfortable silence sat between them like an interloper. Jake knew he'd feel much better about leaving his mum if she could just accept he was going, with or without her approval.

Marion recognised the fear lurking inside her. It was impossible to shake the idea off that, under no circumstances, should Jake return to Bradfield. But she knew, the more she said 'no', the more he'd dig his heels in and go for even longer than he had already threatened. When she'd been younger, Marion could recall there'd been many stand-offs between herself and her own mother. He was more like her than she'd ever realised, she considered, as she watched him grinding his jaw, deep in thought. Maybe it would be okay, after all, Jake was a male adult and Amy had been a vulnerable teenage girl. He'd managed to look after himself pretty well all these years and didn't seem to have turned out too badly.

"Okay, Jake," Marion said eventually, "you win. I don't like it but I realise you feel you need to do this."

Jake beamed. He jumped up from his chair and hugged his mum. "Thank you," he cried. "I promise it'll be fine. I'll be back here, getting in your way again before you know it." He kissed the top of her head, his mind already racing as he made a mental list of things to do.

Chapter 3

Looking up at their old home, Jake wondered whether it had shrunk. He didn't consider himself as being particularly tall, at five feet ten, yet he could see he would have had to bend his head to get through the doorway now.

It stirred up old memories inside his head – the garden was neat and clearly well looked after; a discarded, grubby teddy bear showed Jake it was still a family home of which he was glad. He could almost see himself tearing through the front gate and running down the path at the side of the house to go and play in the back garden, whilst Amy and his mum took the more civilised entrance through the front door.

The paint was beginning to peel on the window frames, but the old, stone cottage still managed to leave a lump in his chest as Jake turned away and walked back to the junction.

He'd got himself a room in a bed and breakfast in High Bradfield and after checking in, despite it being late in the day, Jake had been desperate to take a stroll through his old haunts, just to see what effect it had on him.

His life here, now seemed a lifetime away. Everywhere was so empty and quiet compared to city life. Then, he'd been a child, robbed early of his innocence by what had happened. Growing up had almost occurred overnight as Amy's death had sunk in and splintered their lives. Standing back in the small village as an adult, Jake felt as if he'd walked into a storybook, something he'd read about in years gone by.

Shivering in the twilight, Jake headed uphill towards the B&B. He had a lot more ground to cover but it could wait until morning, he decided.

The hand looked tiny, clasping his own tightly. Normally, such a sight might make a person smile; yet, in his dream, as the hand twisted, the blackened finger tips became visible. Flesh hung loosely from the back of the child's hand and an earthy smell filled Jake's nostrils.

He wanted to scream and run, but the hand clung, possessively to his. Lying on his back, Jake tried to use his other hand to raise himself up but his head hit a rough, hard object, some sort of low ceiling as though he was already entombed. His feet slipped hopelessly against the ground. The atmosphere was damp and clinging to him as stiflingly as the hand.

Feeling the air being squeezed out of his lungs as his panic rose, Jake opened his mouth to yell for help. No sound came out. His eyes blinked quickly as dust particles filtered down onto his face. Turning his head in the direction where the owner of the hand must lie, Jake squinted, peering into the darkness.

"Jake," came the whispered sound of his name, distant but clear. Gradually the sound increased as his name was repeated with an increasing sense of urgency.

He wanted to cover his ears, protect himself against the invading voice. But the onslaught was relentless and his right hand was still immobile.

Suddenly, out of the darkness, a pair of small, brown eyes opened. Maggots fell out of the sockets and Jake was sure he could feel them writhing against the skin of his arm. As he opened his mouth again to scream, a squirming mass seemed to spill from his own mouth as he choked and gagged.

Sitting up abruptly, sweat poured from his body in the dimly lit bedroom. Jake waited whilst his breathing became more regular, his body shaking as the memory of his dream began to fade. Being so used to the nightmares now, and dealing with their effect on him, Jake automatically swung his legs over the side of his bed and picked up the glass of water from the small table. Drinking quickly until the glass was drained and the last drops ran down his chin, Jake could think of one thing only: the eyes he had seen in his nightmare had belonged to Martha. He was positive. So many times, he had found himself staring into those dark pools, mesmerised by their depth, Jake knew he wasn't mistaken. Was it because he was here again? Could it have been his mother's cruel accusations which had put his friend firmly back into his consciousness?

Feeling a little calmer, Jake fell back onto his bed, exhausted. His eyes scanned the simply furnished room but it was as it had been in the daylight.

After that, his sleep was fitful; he woke feeling almost as tired as he had the night before.

The breeziness of his landlady, chatting brightly as she flitted around the floral-decorated breakfast room brought a smile to Jake's face. He could smell bacon and coffee, which was making his mouth water.

She'd relaxed visibly once discovering Jake was originally from the neighbouring village, and appeared duty bound to fill him in on every piece of gossip and news for the last ten years. He nodded or shook his head, as appropriate, dipping in and out of listening to her news stream.

His breakfast was as delicious as the aroma had promised and Jake groaned aloud as he stepped outside onto the pavement, eventually. Being September, the morning had taken a little while to warm up, but the sky was blue, interrupted only by the occasional ball of cotton wool floating across the sun's path.

With the intention of strolling through the woods and making his way up to Martha's familiar address, Jake turned his feet in the direction of the churchyard, where he wished to pay his respects at Amy's graveside, before taking the footpath through the graveyard and into the woods.

His belly was full; a bottle of water and wrapped sandwich from his landlady were secured in his rucksack; the weather was fine; the memory of his nightmare was cast aside as Jake set off smiling to himself.

Today it felt good to be alive, Jake told himself. He'd quite forgotten how beautiful the countryside was in this area, with the rolling hills, a patchwork of fields punctuated with grazing sheep and separated by dry stone walls and small copses. There was already a variety of colours amongst the trees with the nights beginning to draw in and the slight dip in temperature.

Everywhere was peaceful with children ensconced in school; Jake listened to the old, familiar sound of sheep bleating and birdsong as he passed through the tall, metal gateway leading towards St. Nicholas' church.

Pausing to look at the impressive vista which presented itself to him from the churchyard, Jake heard his own intake of breath. The church was perched near the top of the slope and the wide, open valley was spread in front of him. The words of the hymn: All Things Bright and Beautiful, came into Jake's head, although he hadn't heard the tune since primary school. Wondering whether he was about to turn into a poet, Jake grinned, although not before he'd silently dared anyone not to be impressed with the sight he could currently see.

The church was an impressive building, enjoying such a prominent position in the landscape. Its square tower appeared squat in comparison to the length of the nave. Pausing at the stone porch and seeing the church was open, Jake approached the door. He hesitated. The last time he'd been inside, he realised, had been the day of Amy's funeral. Recalling his terror, unsure what was expected of him, clutching his mum's hand tightly, Jake had stared at the sea of dour faces and listened with incomprehension to the words of the service.

The temperature inside was cool. He wandered aimlessly along the aisles, pausing very briefly to read names on plaques until he returned to the door. Shivering as he stepped outside again, the sun's warmth was welcome.

Recalling the location of his sister's grave, Jake suddenly wished he'd had the foresight to bring flowers. There was nothing he could do now, apart from feel as if he was letting Amy down.

He gazed down at the black marble headstone, the letters etched in a silver colour. It was difficult to associate the slab of stone with the girl he remembered. It seemed impersonal, a pebble in the ocean, and a poor reminder of the quiet, thoughtful sister he had known.

Glad he had come, Jake stepped back as his eyes lingered on the mound of grass representing her resting body. Casting his mind back into the distant past, Jake searched his mind for memories of the times he'd spent with his sibling. Although those times had usually been through necessity, or at their mother's insistence they spend some family time together, Jake realised he had no negative recollections of Amy. He found himself wondering what she would be like now, as an adult; would she have had children and a husband?

Her death had been cruel. Amy had loved this land, yet it had treated her with disdain by snatching her young life away so prematurely. It still felt wrong, knowing how well Amy had known the dangers; they had assumed she knew every inch of the hillside where she'd fallen and been fully aware of the risks, seen and unseen. It was hardly surprising their mum's over-riding emotion had been guilt. Having assumed Amy was sensible and accompanied by Patch, there had been no inkling the accident could occur.

Jake had been lucky she'd even let him walk by himself to school after that. Every time he returned home, the relief on his mum's face had been visible.

Casting his eyes round the large graveyard, Jake wondered whether there were ghosts. He had no reason to presume such things were real, but he'd read stories as a child and felt it was inevitable to consider spirits in this vicinity.

With a final glance at Amy's headstone, Jake turned and strolled towards the gate in the wall of the churchyard which led to the woods. Glancing at headstones as he walked, Jake noted some of the writing was illegible, faded with age and green with algae. Other stones were crooked, some broken or fallen, whilst others were new and clean. Dead flowers lay before some, autumn bulbs flowered by others and all the time, the dappled sunlight danced through the leaves, where trees skirted the boundary wall.

The small wooden gate swung closed behind him with a thud against the stone post. The temperature seemed to drop dramatically as the sun became obscured behind a cloud as Jake looked around the woodland. To his right was Bailey Hill, believed to be the site of a Norman castle. He could recall watching Amy scampering over the hilltop with Patch, wondering how she kept her footing on the steep sides. Following the footpath along the side of the hill, Jake glanced between Bailey Hill and the ground falling away to his left amongst the trees. Although this had been Amy's place of sanctuary, Jake had visited the woods occasionally when his mum had forced Amy to accept their company on one of her daily ambles. His memories of the place were hazy but he figured if he stuck to the paths, he'd be fine.

Spying the sky through a gap in the trees, Jake was surprised how grey it now was. He wondered whether he should pop back to the B&B to retrieve his jacket. Then the vision of his landlady, launching into another lengthy round of gossip, made him press on instead.

Leaves danced across in front of him as the wind increased; Jake stepped up his pace, cursing himself again for not automatically bringing a coat out with him and feeling disappointed by this turn in the weather, after having been looking forward to a relaxed stroll.

As the woods opened up into a clearing, Jake paused to get his breath back. He thought he spotted something run across the path in front of him, but couldn't be sure whether it was an animal or small child. His eyes searched the sky; it appeared now as a blanket of grey cloud, unbroken and uninviting. He continued walking, passing through an area of young trees and brush. The woodland ahead seemed to beckon him eagerly as Jake felt his feet speeding forward with the descent of the hill.

Over a stile and back into woodland, the atmosphere darkened again. Jake found himself wondering whether Amy had always enjoyed her visits to the woods, whatever the weather. Certainly, he decided, he was a fair-weather walker.

Crossing a small bridge over a narrow stream, Jake saw the path divided at the far side. He knew he needed to turn right, heading up towards Martha's house and to the left, the woodland became thicker as it weaved down the hill towards Low Bradfield.

The sensation was odd. The coldness in the air was making his feet urgent to get on the path towards Martha's. Yet, something was causing him to pause as if there was a reason for him to travel downhill.

Jake glanced at his watch. It wasn't midday. There was no hurry. Martha wasn't expecting him and might not even be at home. He let his feet lead him downwards as the trees grew denser.

Again, Jake got the impression of someone, or something, crossing the path in front of him. There was an eerie silence as he noted the absence, suddenly, of any birdsong. Even the wind seemed to have ceased, although the sky remained dark and ominous.

Something lurked in the back of Jake's mind. His feet were moving forward automatically, although he wasn't sure whether it was simply that he was following an established footpath. Earlier, he'd been eager to see Martha again, hopeful she would appreciate his unexpected arrival. Now, he felt helpless as his rational thoughts left him, and he blindly walked deeper into the woods.

Unexpectedly, Jake found himself off the path. He was standing in a tangle of brambles, unaware of how he had found his way to their centre. As he lifted each leg in turn, thorns tore at his jeans; grateful his legs were protected from the small, sharp spikes, Jake's eyes searched for the direction of the path.

There was no sign of it. Surrounded by brambles, ferns and trees, the ground was a mass of dead leaves. Again, the sound of scurrying feet carried to his ears. His head darted in all directions, yet he appeared to be alone.

Reminding himself it was the middle of the day, Jake took great strides across the strands of bramble. His progress was slow as he untangled the plants from their hold on his jeans. Unsure of which direction he was now moving in, Jake paused often and listened for signs of civilisation, aware in his head of the location of his destination in relation to the road; he hoped to hear the familiar sound of vehicles.

The sound of a scream was accompanied by the sudden flapping of wings as birds took flight. Could the cry have come from a bird? Jake wondered, recovering from the fright of the unexpected noise. He stopped moving and listened.

Silence. Then, a gradual increase in the wind as it whipped between the trees. Its progress built quickly until leaves were whirling above the ground. Again, the sound of a scream. Jake's head moved round quickly as he looked for the source. A shadow darted between two spindly trees which groaned in the wind. They were too narrow to shield anyone, but Jake could see nothing.

His heart was racing. He closed his eyes as dirt was thrown up from the ground with the leaves, which stabbed at his hands and face like tiny pins. Raising his arm to protect his eyes, Jake peered ahead of him. The wind was gaining in strength. He could see something lying on the ground ahead of him; if nothing else, he thought, he could shelter against it until the breeze subsided.

The thorns pulled at his legs. He staggered slowly towards his destination whilst the air turned almost as black as night. Surely, he would have seen a warning on the news if a storm had been expected, Jake considered, cursing his lack of protection from the elements again. Certainly, he would have presumed his landlady would have known if he needed to be better equipped to deal with a sudden downturn in the weather. He may not be as expert as Amy had been, but Jake had the sense to realise the dangers of being ill-equipped to deal with the harshness of an exposed site in a storm.

Pushing forward, head bowed against the wind, Jake kept moving, albeit slowly until he dropped to his knees by the side of a large, fallen tree trunk. Exhausted, Jake leant his forehead against the ancient wood before swinging himself round to sit with his back resting against the trunk.

As his breath calmed, Jake was relieved by the respite from the howling gale in the sheltered position he found himself in. Looking around him, aware of the sound of creaking and cracking wood, he pushed his back against the tree. His hand slipped down into a space beneath the trunk. Sweeping away the pine needles and leaves which carpeted the ground, Jake peered down into the hole he'd revealed. It appeared to be an empty space, Jake assumed an animal had burrowed down into the earth to create a home.

Whilst looking into the gap, the sound of an almighty roar split the air as a nearby tree groaned under the strength of the wind. Instinctively, Jake let his body fall sideways, just as the tree dropped, falling across the trunk he lay behind.

Twigs, leaves and dirt showered around him, but, with the exception of a few minor cuts, Jake was unharmed. Shaking, he slid his body out from under the broken branches and pulled himself up using the trunk for support. He saw immediately, how close he'd come to having his skull smashed by the fallen tree.

The wind battered against his head. His eyes stung with the effort of trying to peer around him. Believing he caught a glimpse of a moving figure, Jake raised his hand in the air. His arm was battered and blown backwards and forwards, despite his muscles being tensed.

And then, quite suddenly, the gale ceased. Jake fell against the trunk with the release of pressure. Shocked, he pushed himself upright and slowly turned. With the exception of the newly fallen tree, there was no evidence of the storm he'd just experienced.

Before Jake could begin to consider what had happened, he heard the sound of running feet. Spinning round, a boisterous Labrador appeared by his side, tail wagging and a long, pink tongue lolling out of the side of its mouth.

A whistle sounded in the distance but the dog ignored it, instead choosing to sniff the ground next to Jake's feet.

From behind a tree, a girl approached them, cursing quietly but continuously. She came to an abrupt halt when she spotted Jake.

He couldn't help but stare at her; she was the spitting image of Amy. If it wasn't for the fact Amy would now be a woman in her mid-twenties, this teenager looked just as his sister had when he'd last seen her alive. Okay, Amy wouldn't have dreamt of wearing the scruffy leather jacket, or having the facial piercings this girl wore, but she looked like Amy, nonetheless.

Realising she was beginning to back away from him, Jake apologised, spluttering like a fool as he dragged his eyes away from her.

"I'm really sorry," he repeated. "You look so much like someone I used to know."

She looked at him as if he was crazy. "Whatever," she drawled, slapping her hand against her leg until the dog trotted to her side.

"Can you tell me which direction it is to High Bradfield?" Jake asked as she began to step backwards again.

For a moment she paused, head cocked slightly to one side. There was something about this guy, she thought, creepy – yes; finding him just standing in the middle of the woods like that, evidently up to no-good. Yet, there was something else, something she couldn't put her finger on … maybe she had seen him somewhere before? Then shaking her head, the girl pointed to her right before hurrying off in the opposite direction. Jake heard a single word shouted over her shoulder as she disappeared from sight: "Pervert!"

A laugh escaped from Jake's lips as he leant his bum against the trunk. What on earth had just happened? First, the storm whipping up out of nowhere, then, almost being crushed by a falling tree, before a girl who looked exactly like his dead sister, had assumed he was doing something dodgy in the woods.

Jake pulled his rucksack off his back and rummaged inside it for his water bottle. Drinking the cool liquid in long gulps, Jake closed his eyes. In that brief moment, the remembrance of his nightmare from the previous night, flashed into his mind. His eyes shot open and he swore when a slug of water dropped down the front of his shirt.

Now he was spooking himself. Of course, being in some woods was bound to remind him of his dream, yet he still noted the unsteadiness of his breathing as he put the bottle away and slung the rucksack onto his back.

Could he have just dreamt it all? No, he thought, the storm had set in before he'd laid on the ground. It had arrived as soon as he'd re-entered the woods after crossing the bridge.

Testing the steadiness of his legs, Jake leaned forward before moving off and heading in the direction the girl had pointed. Once he was out of the brambles, Jake quickly found the path. He could only hope she had given him the right information.

As he walked, Jake thought about the girl; her likeness to Amy was uncanny. Although clearly trying to appear older, it had been evident she was still of school age. She hadn't appeared dishevelled or alarmed by the storm; now, as he began to think about the storm, Jake looked around him as he walked. There were no broken trees, no fallen branches and no sign of disorder. It was suddenly like he'd imagined the whole thing, as he found himself back at the crossroads with the bridge.

Jake stood still. Slowly he turned in a full circle. It was impossible. Here, there had been no storm. He shuddered. It was tempting to hurry back to the B&B, pack his things and leave. However, as his mind turned to thoughts of Martha, Jake put one foot in front of the other and headed on, up the hill resolutely.

Chapter 4

Angrily, Jake blinked back tears of frustration. No good acting like a girl now, he told himself. Man up and sort yourself out before you see Martha or she'll be slamming the door in your face.

At the top of the slope, Jake paused at a stile, peering into the field beyond, uncertain now of which way he needed to go. Across the grassy slope, he could just make out the roof of a building; that had to be Martha's place, he decided.

Sitting down on top of the stile, Jake pulled his sandwiches out of his pack and quickly took a bite, suddenly realising how ravenous he was.

As he ate, Jake looked around him. Yes, he could still appreciate how beautiful everywhere looked; but today, for the first time, he had also seen how threatening it could be too. Clearly, he wasn't an outdoor kind of person like Amy had been.

Jake wondered what the girl's name had been; it would be even weirder if she was called Amy as well.

He screwed up the foil and threw it back into his rucksack. Jumping down into the field, Jake took a deep breath. Either this was going to go great and he and Martha would have a lot of catching up to do, or his surprise would fall flat on its face and he would look like an idiot.

Standing on the side of the road and looking at the bungalow at the end of the driveway, Jake paused. He'd only seen this place as a ruin, before Martha's folks had bought it and done it up; he'd never visited her here when they had still lived in the village, his mum would have gone spare.

Now, it wasn't that different in appearance to how he had pictured it in his mind: okay, there was glass in the windows and it had a roof on, but it looked pretty sorry for itself. The garden was a mass of weeds and strangled plants; a couple of the roof tiles had slipped out of place; and it just had a general unloved and uncared-for kind of feel.

This had to be the right bungalow. It had been several years since they had exchanged letters, with the internet being much more convenient, but Martha had never said she'd moved house.

Strolling up the drive, dodging the broken slabs, towards the front door, Jake knew the only thing he could do was to give it a go. With more confidence than he felt, Jake rapped his knuckles against the door. He waited, listening.

With no response forthcoming, Jake knocked again. He'd not made a contingency plan; in his imagination, Martha had opened the door at once and welcomed him with a hug.

Stepping back from the door, Jake decided to see if there was another entrance. At the corner of the bungalow he came to a fence and gate. The latch lifted at his touch; cautiously, he pushed the gate open and stepped into the backyard.

It had once been a large patio, Jake decided. Now, most of the slabs were broken, weeds and grass pushing up through the gaps. Rusty garden tools lay, abandoned on the ground, a shed stood, with it door open, gently swinging backwards and forwards, the interior empty apart from a half empty bag of compost.

Looking at the building, Jake noted the back door was open. From inside came the sound of music. As he moved closer, he recognised it as an old war-time, big band tune, Glen Miller, he presumed. He smiled to himself as he realised the sound was scratchy, like a record.

Leaning on the door frame, Jake called: "Hello? Martha?"

There was a scuffling noise and then footsteps on a hard surface approaching. She stopped at the doorway on the far side of the kitchen and stared at him.

"Jake?"

Not sure what else to say, Jake simply nodded.

"Oh my god," Martha added, taking the sight of him in. She stepped forward, smiling.

"It's okay I came then?" he asked, still standing outside.

She nodded, her hands clasped in front of her mouth.

He realised they probably looked like a pair of love-sick teenagers, each just staring at the other, too tongue-tied to speak.

"You gonna invite me in then, or should we just stand here?" Jake asked eventually.

For a moment, Martha hesitated as her eyes scanned the kitchen; it was a state, she knew. Then she shrugged and nodding, beckoned him in.

Jake ignored their surroundings and held his arms open. Martha walked straight into his embrace.

She smelt of lavender, he thought, as he held her. It felt comfortable and good, much easier than when they'd been children.

The music stopped and the sound of a record spinning with the needle running repeatedly over the end of the disc travelled through from somewhere inside the bungalow.

"I was worried the surprise might fall flat," Jake told her. He wanted to look at her face but she held on around his waist, her head pressed against his chest. He was slightly embarrassed: glad she was pleased to see him, but wanting to chat and catch up as old friends in a relaxed way.

"You gonna let go?" Jake asked eventually, becoming too warm with his rucksack still on his back.

Martha gave a small giggle, before sweeping back her long, dark hair from her face as she took a step back. "I'm sorry," she sighed, looking up at his face. "I just can't believe you're really here, after so long."

Jake smiled. She was much shorter than he was, perhaps only five feet. Her hair hung in loose curls and he felt his heart lurch at the sight of those dark brown eyes, sparkling now as she watched him. "I know, I thought about letting you know my plans, but then I decided it would be nice to surprise you; you don't seem to mind too much?"

"No!" Martha cried. "It's great to see you; how long has it been?"

"About ten years," Jake replied. "This is the first time I've been back."

"Is your mum here too?" Martha suddenly asked, peering behind Jake into the garden.

"No," he replied. "I left her at home, thought I'd come back and check the place out, see if it was still the same."

"And is it?" she asked, smiling.

Jake looked at her. Once the vision of the small schoolgirl disappeared from his head and he saw the young woman standing before him, he grinned. "Some things have changed."

Martha knew what he meant immediately. "For the better?" she asked, hand on hip.

"Definitely for the better," he beamed, as his eyes devoured the sight of her body: shirt opened seductively showing the slight rise of her breasts; corduroy short skirt revealing slim legs; oh, and those eyes, he sighed again to himself. Jake was certainly glad he'd made the effort to come here, after all.

Suddenly, Martha tore her eyes away from Jake and stepped behind him into the kitchen. "Can I get you some tea?"

Jake let his bag slide to the floor. He noted the concrete beneath their feet; Martha's feet were bare, it couldn't be good to walk on.

"Um, yeah, okay," he answered. For the first time, as she filled the kettle and stood it on the hob to boil, Jake looked around them.

The place was a sight! Work surfaces were stained and covered in piles of crockery and pans. An old-fashioned fridge filled an entire corner. Cupboard doors hung open showing empty interiors, evidently, housework wasn't one of Martha's strengths.

He kicked his bag to the edge of the room. The sound seemed to make Martha jump and she turned around.

"Sorry," Jake sighed, pointing to his bag.

Martha smiled and fetched the milk from the fridge. For such a huge beast, it only showed a couple of things on its shelves. Then she picked up numerous cups, peering in each one. Eventually satisfied, she placed two cups on floral saucers, it reminded Jake of his landlady, a woman who must be in her seventies or even eighties.

With the cups on a tray, complete with teapot, sugar bowl and milk jug, Martha picked it up: "Should we?" she asked, nodding towards the open doorway.

Jake smiled politely. "After you."

Following Martha down a bare hallway, the floor here just concrete too, Jake glanced into the rooms they passed. All seemed devoid of decoration and furniture, only the essentials. It didn't look like a home, but a house waiting to be sold. Jake was surprised and slightly concerned; he didn't like to think of Martha in this place, although her emails had sounded cheerful enough.

She'd disappeared into a room and Jake followed. Wow, he thought, this was a bit different. The walls were covered in a wallpaper, decorated with small rosebuds; the floor, whilst not carpeted, at least had a linoleum base. The sideboard, bookcases and coffee table were matching, a dark wood, and a three-piece suite of deep pink velvet, looking worn but comfortable, greeted them. In the corner stood a small table with a gramophone on top, surrounded by piles of old records.

Jake couldn't help staring, open-mouthed. It was like they'd stepped back in time to the fifties, or even earlier. The books lining the bookcases had dark spines and the photographs were all in black and white, sitting in tarnished silver frames. He knew some people liked retro, but this was taking things a bit far, he thought.

When he glanced at Martha, Jake was disconcerted to see she was staring at him. He recalled suddenly, from childhood, it was a habit of hers, as though she was absorbing a person's thoughts.

He mustered a smile which she quickly returned.

"Take a seat," she sang, indicating the sofa, filled with crocheted cushions.

Jake sat in one of the armchairs, resting his arms lightly on the arms. He watched as Martha set a record on the deck and then went about pouring their tea.

"Sugar?" she asked, tongs in hand.

Jake shook his head. "Just a dash of milk."

The strains of another big band tune filled the air, the scratchy sound discordant to his ears.

Martha placed his cup and saucer on the coffee table in front of him. Jake pulled himself forward, waiting for her to join him.

Martha took a seat in the middle of the sofa and straightened out creases he couldn't see in her skirt. Eventually she stopped, folded her hands in her lap and smiled at him. "Isn't this nice?"

"Lovely," Jake lied. He didn't think he could feel more uncomfortable. This atmosphere was so different to when she had first greeted him. Having had time to get used to the idea of his being here, it was as if she was now playing a role.

"You get on alright, up here on your own?" Jake asked, desperate to fill the silence with small talk.

The bungalow was isolated, a mile uphill from High Bradfield. The views were amazing but it was at a junction in the roads and Jake was sure it could be pretty lonely in the depths of winter.

Originally, when she'd moved to the village, Jake seemed to recall she'd lived with her gran and dad. He knew her gran had died a long time ago. Martha's dad had died a while ago too, killed in an accident at work. Jake knew there'd been an insurance pay out which meant she managed as far as money was concerned.

Martha looked around the room, smiling. "Oh, it's just fine," she cooed. "I like my records, as you can see."

Jake looked at the piles. "You must have hundreds."

"Thousands," she corrected. "There's more in the bedroom."

"Don't you get lonely?" he asked.

Martha frowned. "Lonely?"

"Yeah, you know, living in this place with no one else?"

She appeared surprised by his question. Jake knew he wouldn't fancy it.

"I don't have time to get lonely: I have my books and my records," she replied, indicating the things around them.

Jake smiled and picked up his cup. Something floated at the edge of the tea, Jake turned it, keeping his eyes on the unidentified thing floating in his drink. He grimaced: it tasted bland.

"I will have a sugar," he said, smiling as he put his cup back on the saucer.

Eagerly, Martha stood up and dropped a lump into his cup.

"Thanks," Jake said, picking up the teaspoon and stirring his drink.

"So, what are your plans whilst you're here?" Martha asked. "Have you got somewhere to stay? I can find space here, but it would only be a sleeping bag on the floor, I'm afraid," she said keenly.

"Ah, no, you're fine," he replied hastily. "I'm in a B&B in High Bradfield, just along from the church."

Martha nodded and gazed out of the window.

Jake followed her eyes to the large picture window, stiff net curtains hung in the window which was framed by a long pair of pink curtains which matched the colour of the suite. It was all a bit pink for his liking.

"Do you ever see anyone else we were at school with?" Jake asked, as Martha continued staring.

She shook her head slightly. "Sorry?"

"I just wondered whether you saw anyone who went to school with us in the village."

She appeared surprised by his question. "No."

"Oh." Jake noted how relaxed she appeared. Compared to his own ill-ease, he wished he could match her comfortable calm. "You like all this retro stuff?" He asked, searching his brain for things to say.

"Retro?" Martha laughed. "It's hardly old, Jake."

For a moment, he assumed she was joking and began to laugh too; then, seeing her perfectly composed expression, he realised she was genuinely surprised by his assumption and stopped himself.

"Sorry," he said quickly. "Hope I didn't offend you; it just looks different to my mum's stuff."

"I'll make us a fresh pot," Martha said, pointing at the teapot. She jumped up and left him alone.

Listening to the sounds of her pottering in the kitchen, Jake got up and picked up one of the photographs from a shelf. There was a thin layer of dust across the surface, but it was still clear it was old. He peered at the small faces. They all looked serious, no smiles for the camera. He recognised a picture of Martha as a child; she was sitting on the lap of a woman, he assumed was her mum. Martha was wearing a cloak and a pair of tiny boots which looked almost Victorian in style.

"This your mum?" Jake asked as she came back.

Martha nodded and smiled. She sat down, so Jake returned to his chair as she topped up his cup.

He wondered how soon he could respectfully make his excuses and leave. Feeling disappointed, Jake cursed himself for having assumed the lost years would just disappear and they would be able to pick up where they'd left off ten years earlier. It was evident they had matured into very different people. He belonged in a city now and was part of the twenty first century. Martha seemed to have been caught up in time, still living in her childhood home which looked like a museum.

"You don't like it, do you?"

Jake looked across at her face, worried that she'd somehow read his thoughts.

Seeing she didn't appear offended, Jake smiled. "Sorry, just not my style."

"Fancy a walk?" She asked.

Trying not to let his relief show too evidently, Jake nodded. He even took a huge gulp of his tea before following her into the kitchen.

Jake picked up his rucksack, whilst Martha pulled on a pair of wellies and fed her arms into the sleeves of a thick, woollen cardigan.

She locked the door behind them and Jake led the way back round to the road. "Where to?" he asked as she came to a standstill by his side.

"This way," Martha replied, linking her hand through his arm and pulling him in the direction he'd come earlier.

Jake hesitated as she passed through the kissing gate which led back across the field towards the woods. Then, watching her striding through the long grass, he shrugged, took a deep breath and followed.

Running to catch up with her, Jake was taken aback by the warm smile with which she greeted him. Feeling himself relax, he fed her hand through his arm again. Martha leaned across and gave him a quick peck on the cheek, then looked hurriedly away.

When they reached the junction of footpaths by the bridge, Martha looked in the various directions: "Any preference?" she asked.

"I'd rather not go down to the woods," Jake replied.

"Up on the hill?" Martha asked, pointing through the trees.

Jake shuddered. "No," he replied quickly.

"Oh sorry," she muttered. "Of course, Amy …"

His sister's name hung in the air between them. The hill was where Amy had fallen, receiving her fatal injuries.

"I guess, it's this way then!" Martha exclaimed and headed to the bridge.

They wandered slowly back up towards Bailey Hill, mostly in silence with the occasional comment passing between them. It felt natural, Jake was relieved to realise, after the awkwardness he'd felt in her home.

At the foot of the Hill, Martha came to a standstill and turned to face Jake. She held out her hand towards him which he accepted in his. She pulled him to her until their faces were just inches apart.

"Would you like to kiss me?" she whispered.

Jake gave a small laugh, then saw she was serious. Instead of replying, he gave her a peck on the lips. As he pulled back, he saw Martha still stood with her eyes closed. After a brief hesitation, Jake pressed his lips against hers. She tasted of cherries, he decided. As Martha returned his kiss, Jake realised his body was responding more quickly than he would have liked and pulled back from her again.

Her eyes sparkled as she watched him. "Did you enjoy that?" she asked, as though she already knew the answer.

Jake smiled and shook his hand free of hers before turning around and walking away.

"I know you did," Martha called after him. "I felt you getting hard." She giggled.

When Jake turned around, she was nowhere to be seen. He'd been shocked by her bluntness, and was rather self-conscious. Martha's mood appeared to be able to turn in a flash. Where was she now?

He followed the path leading around the base of the Hill. A flurry, as a pheasant flew up from the undergrowth, made him jump. Jake could feel the irritation growing inside him.

"Martha!" he yelled.

Apart from the echo of his own voice: nothing. Sod this, Jake thought to himself; she's clearly happy to lead him on and then waltz off. Well, he wasn't about to make a complete idiot of himself. Turning heel, Jake strode off, walking quickly until he reached the churchyard. Was she a prick teaser, or was Martha really so innocent she had no idea what she was doing to him?

Slowing his pace then, he'd expected Martha to come chasing after him, but nothing. He put his head down and walked past the church, through the gate and along the cobbled road until he reached the B&B.

As he opened the front door, Jake glanced back down the road. Martha stood in the centre of the road watching him. After just a moment's hesitation, Jake pushed the door open and went inside.

It was definitely Amy's voice but the sound was distorted. Had she called his name? Jake couldn't be certain. As usual, everywhere smelt of damp soil; it was suffocating.

Hands came out of the darkness, clawing at his body and face. Twisting and turning, Jake tried in vain to throw them off. He felt himself slipping downwards; his feet and hands pressed into the ground to prevent his fall but the soil just dropped away, building an avalanche of dirt which showered him.

As the edge of the drop seemed to rise to greet him, Jake looked helplessly skyward. Silhouetted against the fading light was Amy; she was standing on a hill: Bailey Hill and her finger was pointing. As Jake felt his body begin to plummet, he realised the direction his sister had been pointing towards and knew where she needed him to go.

The following morning, disturbed by his dream but inexplicably scared of the thought of returning to the woods after what had happened there the previous day, Jake decided he would see if Martha would go with him. Of course, he wasn't about to let her know of his fears, he didn't want her to think he was gutless.

She acted as if their parting the preceding day had been perfectly amicable, seemingly expecting to see him again. They walked across the field and Jake waited until they reached the bridge before suggesting they continue straight ahead.

Initially Martha appeared surprised, but said nothing and they continued into the woods. The path was too narrow for them to walk side by side; Jake walked a little behind, watching Martha's petite figure. It wasn't until they arrived at the fallen tree that Jake realised she had brought them to the spot without him needing to tell her where he wanted to go.

He looked at her in amazement: "How did you know this was the place?"

Her expression changed from confusion to indignation. "What do you mean? I just stopped so you could say where we were heading."

Jake frowned. It was a bit of a coincidence. "Well, this is it!"

Martha scowled, her brow creased in a deep furrow. "What do you mean? What game are you playing, Jake?"

Her anger seemed unnecessary. "My game! What's the matter with you?" Jake asked.

"Is this why you came back? Did your mum put you up to this?" Her voice was screeching, higher and higher.

"What are you going on about? What's my mum got to do with anything?" Jake was at a loss.

"You brought me to this place on purpose," Martha stated. "Is she here? Hiding? With her stupid little threats and theories again?"

As Martha scanned the surrounding area, fists clenched by her sides, Jake searched his mind for some explanation.

"Martha," he began at length. "For goodness sake, calm down. I've no idea why you're getting yourself worked up like this. I thought we were just coming out for a walk. I thought I knew where we were going," he lied, "but it doesn't matter. I'm sure you know these woods far better than I do."

"Why should I know them better? It's your mum, I know this is her doing. She just couldn't let things be."

"That's it!" Jake cried. "Leave my mum out of this. Are you going to tell me what your problem is, or not?"

Her face was crimson. Jake was hurt by her inexplicable attack on his mother. He knew his mum had a dislike of Martha but he'd never realised it was mutual.

"I thought you were my friend, Jake," Martha began quietly. "I thought you were the one person in this world I could completely trust. How stupid I was; I should've known better."

As she started to walk away, Jake put out his hand and grabbed her arm.

"Hey! Don't just go. Tell me what's wrong. I have no idea why you're angry with me; what am I supposed to have done?"

Martha glared at him. Her eyes fiery. "How dare you bring me here, Jake Brooks? I don't ever want to see you again." With that, Martha turned heel and took off, almost at a running pace, disappearing whilst Jake stared after her.

He was stunned. Her anger had appeared out of nowhere and Jake had no idea what he was supposed to have done which had clearly upset her so much. Evidently, there was no point going after her now; Martha needed time to calm down, but he would get to the bottom of this.

Slowly, Jake turned, gazing at the woods around him. All was still and quiet. He decided to continue down the hill towards Low Bradfield. By the time he got there, it would be lunchtime. He intended to have a pint at the pub, perhaps he'd get a bus into Sheffield for the afternoon. His visit to the village of his childhood wasn't turning out to be quite as nostalgic as he'd hoped.

A stroll around the city centre, followed by an early dinner helped to improve his spirits. Jake smiled to himself as he sat on the bus heading back to the B&B. Being amongst the crowds in the city had helped remind Jake that his life was generally good and if he chose, he could head home whenever he wanted. He'd decided he'd give Martha a couple of days to calm down, then, if she still refused to have anything to do with him, he'd leave her here with the rest of his past, and return to his life further north.

The queue of traffic meant the bus didn't reach the village until after dark. Assuming there had been an accident, Jake dozed for the last part of the journey. It was only when they came to a halt at the bus stop, he noticed the abundance of police vehicles parked along the kerb.

Curiosity raised, Jake slipped into the pub, rather than going straight to the B&B. It was certainly busier than he'd expected for a Tuesday evening. Making his way eventually to the bar, Jake ordered a pint of ale and asked the bar tender what was going on as he paid for his drink.

"Apparently, they've found the missing girl's body, up in the woods. Cops everywhere, it's cordoned off."

Jake nodded his thanks and slid back into the crowd to allow someone else to take his place at the bar. He looked for somewhere to perch whilst he drank his pint.

"Jake?"

Turning at the sound of his name, Jake spotted someone waving in his direction. He pushed his way through the crowd to where the bloke sat at the corner of a table.

"Jake Brooks?" he repeated.

Jake nodded, trying to look apologetic, not recognising who was speaking to him.

"It's me, Richard Taylor; we were at primary school together, remember?"

Jake searched his mind, listening to the sound of the name in his head. Suddenly, the penny dropped: "Richard Taylor, of course."

They shook hands, each eyeing the other carefully.

"How you doin', mate?" Richard asked.

"Yeah, fine, sorry, I didn't recognise you, been a long time. We've both changed a bit!" Jake laughed.

"Yeah, but I thought it was you as soon as you walked in," Richard told him. "You live around here still?"

Jake shook his head. Their voices were raised against the din of all the conversations around them. "This is the first time I've been back in ten years," he told Richard. "I've only seen Martha so far."

"You mean: Weird Martha?"

Jake frowned. "Weird?"

"Yeah, you must remember what she was like? Fine one minute, fighting the next. Didn't seem to care whether it was a girl or a boy; she was like a spitting cat. She still live up at the top?" Richard nodded his head in the directions of the bungalow.

Jake nodded. "There on her own," he replied, knowingly.

"Not surprised," Richard replied. "Have to be a brave man to take her on, I reckon."

Smiling, Jake simply rolled his eyes. He wasn't about to admit to his attraction towards Martha. His own body seemed to roll between longing and caution, as far as she was concerned.

"You here for long?" Richard asked.

Jake shrugged. "Depends," he replied vaguely. "What's the story with you?"

Richard filled Jake in on the last ten years of his life. He still lived with his parents in Low Bradfield. He'd always wanted to be a journalist so juggled a part-time job at a local paper with a college course. He was clearly excited by all the police attention around the place, hoping his local knowledge might give him the edge for a good story.

He told Jake the police had descended during the afternoon quite suddenly, cordoning off the entrances to the woods at once. There had been numerous vehicles coming and going ever since but no statement had yet been made.

There was a raised feeling of anticipation amongst local residents, as well as loitering members of the press. Jake was relieved he hadn't gone straight back to the B&B, he could imagine his landlady waiting to pounce on him as soon as he got in with so much excitement in the air.

In unison, everyone cast their eyes towards the door whenever it opened as the buzz of conversation dimmed. But there was no news forthcoming all evening and reluctantly, people headed homewards.

Jake opened the front door of the B&B as quietly as he could. Hearing the sound of a television in the landlady's sitting room, he tiptoed upstairs. At the creak of the final step, he launched himself into his room as quickly as he could, closing the door behind him.

His dream was the same as the previous night: Amy stood on top of the hill. He was falling one minute, buried in another, both Martha's and Amy's faces came at him out of the darkness from opposite sides, each vying for his attention. Jake's head filled with their voices, beating out a rhythm of his name.

Then, quite suddenly, their voices began to fade as the sky grew red. A tree silhouetted against the horizon, a body hanging – long, damp hair covered the face; a long, dirty skirt clung to the body's legs; small feet just inches from the ground pointing downwards.

Like a speeded-up film, Jake watched silently, helplessly, as time passed and the body began to rot. Crows circled overhead and all the while, the sky remained angry.

A crash brought Jake abruptly back to reality. Listening for further sounds, he felt the sweat on his chest, heaving as his breath slowly became calmer.

Glancing at the face of his watch, lying on the table by his bed, Jake noted it wasn't yet 7am. He lay his head back onto the pillow and tried to relax his brain into slumber.

At breakfast, his landlady was eager to inform him that the police had confirmed a body had been discovered in the woods, believed to be that of the missing girl. She seemed quite oblivious to his discomfort as the memory of being informed about the discovery of his sister's body in the same woods crept into Jake's mind. He recalled the knocks on the door and the whispered conversations; the police uniforms and the inhuman wail from his mother's mouth. It had passed in a haze at the time, and was surreal now as time appeared to replay the past.

Needing some fresh air once he'd eaten, Jake donned his jacket and walking boots, before slinging his rucksack onto his back and heading down towards Low Bradfield.

There were people everywhere: police manning cordoned off areas, talking to those standing around, other officers and forensic team members passed backwards and forwards through the barriers. Members of the public and press loitered, hoping for some news, or simply wishing to be present as part of the circus.

Pausing only briefly, Jake scanned the crowd, hoping to catch a glimpse of Richard. Unable to see him immediately, he pushed his way past them and headed away from the woods and the village; he didn't mind where his feet took him, as long as it was away from everyone else.

Finding himself at a reservoir, Jake decided to skirt the perimeter. The air had an autumnal chilliness to it so he was glad of the plan and focused on following the gravel path.

Ducks and moorhens bobbed on the water which alternately sparkled with dappled sunlight or suddenly plummeted to the darkest shades of blue and black. Leaves fluttered to the ground like confetti ahead of him and Jake found himself beginning to relax. Coming across a bench, overlooking the reservoir, Jake took a seat, leaning against his backpack and closing his eyes briefly.

A light breeze brushed across his face. Jake opened his eyes and took in his surroundings. It was tranquil, so very different to what was happening now, back in the village. He thought about the girl's family: their relief, yet also the grief they would now share.

Was it coincidence? The death of his sister and, now, this girl, both found in the same woods. His sister had fallen from a hilltop and, somehow, managed to drag herself to the woods where her body had been found. Had she been trying to make her way home? That was the theory at the time. Now, it seemed to lose some of its reliability as an explanation, as far as Jake was concerned. Why had Amy taken herself back to the woods? Surely it would have made sense to stay put and wait for help to arrive or to have taken herself down to one of the nearby farms. What was the significance of the woods? Was there a significance, or was he becoming fanciful? Perhaps it was the effect of being back here, after so long. Maybe he was looking for a reason to justify Amy's death, just as his mother had been doing, all these years.

Certainly, Jake knew he couldn't let himself become obsessed as she had been; one of them had to keep a rational head on their shoulders.

Briefly, Jake thought about Martha. Was she still angry with him? After remaining friends all this time, it would be foolish to let their friendship drop now; he would stick to his plan and give her a bit of cooling off time.

Picking up his rucksack, Jake continued on the path around the water until he came back to his starting point. On an impulse, he walked just as far as the bus stop and got on the next bus to the city. He knew he needed to keep himself occupied and away from the furore in the village.

As before, his outing served its purpose: the buzz of city life buoyed Jake's spirits and the memory of the girl's death, as well as thoughts about Amy and Martha faded from his mind. He even hung round to eat before catching a later bus back to the village.

Early the next morning, Jake was woken by the sound of knocking. Groggily he sat up, rubbed his eyes and stretched before opening the door.

A man wearing a jacket, shirt and jeans held up a police identification badge. "Jake Brooks?"

Jake nodded, then added: "Yes."

"My name's Detective Cameron. I'd like you to accompany me as there are some questions I'd like to ask you."

Jake frowned, still holding the door handle. "Questions?"

"Yes. If you'd like to get dressed, I'll wait for you downstairs."

Watching the officer disappear back down the stairs before he could respond, Jake closed the door, his head fizzing. What on earth would they want to question him about?

In a daze, he pulled on his clothes, splashed some water on his face and tried to make himself look respectable. Maybe it was about the similarities surrounding his sister's death and that of this girl? It could be they were hoping he could share some of his own experience with the police, or the family of the girl?

Feeling a little more relaxed, yet still curious, Jake went downstairs where the detective was waiting in the hall, cup and saucer in hand, whilst the landlady chattered away to him.

At the sound of Jake's footsteps on the stairs, they both turned. The officer handed his cup back and thanked her. Jake was very aware of the look of disapproval she cast in his direction as he followed the policeman out of the house and into the waiting squad car.

Chapter 5

The formality was intimidating enough, without the scene he'd seen so many times on television playing itself out in front of him, with himself playing the lead role.

The bare room, with just a table and four chairs, a recording device on the table and overhead light, was cold. Jake wondered whether there was a viewing room with numerous other people invisibly watching them.

Feeling childlike, he answered the initial questions ascertaining his identity. Detective Cameron stared at Jake blankly. His companion, another male, leaned back in his chair, arms folded, presumably in the room just to make up numbers. He seemed quite indifferent to what was going on.

Jake felt the sweat in the palms of his hands. He'd refused the offer of a cup of coffee, not wishing them to see how much his hands would be shaking when he tried to lift the drink to his mouth.

"Now, Mr Brooks, Jake if I may?"

Jake nodded.

"Can you tell us why you were in the woods on the morning of the 14th?" His cheek twitched as he waited for Jake to speak.

"The 14th?" Jake couldn't have said what day of the week today was, yet alone the date in the month.

"Yes. The day before yesterday: Tuesday."

Jake ignored his irritation at the man's tone. Was it his fault if he didn't keep up with the date when he was supposed to be on holiday?

"I went for a walk,' he confessed. "I haven't been here for ten years; I just wanted to take a stroll and see the old haunts. My sister died here, you see, and I was only ten at the time. I didn't know how much I would be able to remember."

Detective Cameron's eyebrow was raised. Jake felt like a schoolboy sitting before his headmaster not being believed about his role in some prank.

"We've been informed that your behaviour was rather odd, not that of someone simply taking a morning walk." He leaned further across the table, his eyes not leaving Jake's.

Jake imagined he could feel the detective's breath on his face. This must be what an inquisition must feel like, he thought. They might as well have a spot light aimed at him and thumb screws on the desk. He couldn't feel any more guilty, yet was unaware of his crime.

"Odd? I'm sorry, I don't know what you mean," Jake admitted.

"We have a witness, Jake. She saw you in the woods on the morning of the 14th and found your behaviour suspicious; I believe she actually described it as 'frightening'."

Although he knew he was innocent of any crime, Jake felt the colour draining from his face. Of course, it must be the girl who looked like Amy. He recalled the weird weather he'd experienced. Would the police believe him if he told them about the storm? Jake doubted it. He was quickly gaining the impression this man wasn't going to believe anything he said.

"Do you have anything to say?" The detective prompted.

"I can't think why my behaviour might have appeared frightening," Jake began. "I went for a walk, I thought I knew the way but realised I was lost. For a moment, I panicked. I think I know the girl who spoke to you, she looked exactly like my sister, Amy." He looked at the policemen, for some confirmation that they agreed. Anyone who had seen photographs of his sister would be aware of the likeness to this girl; they clearly knew all about Amy and what had happened to her. "It's possible she came across me when I'd lost the path, but certainly, the shock of her appearance did take me by surprise."

Detective Cameron shook his head slowly. For the first time he took his eyes from Jake's face and glanced at his companion. They exchanged a whispered conversation before their attention returned to Jake.

"I see from our notes, in the case of your sister's death, your mother was convinced at the time, of some foul play."

Jake ran his hands through his hair. He recalled his mum's erratic behaviour, along with her theories of Amy's death being impossible as an accident.

"My mum was understandably, devastated by Amy's death," Jake began calmly. "She would have accepted any explanation other than the truth. Who would want to believe that their teenage daughter had 'accidentally' fallen to her death whilst she was unsupervised? Amy knew the woods and hills better than the inside of our cottage. Of course she shouldn't have fallen to her death out there." His hands were shaking and his blood was racing through his veins.

"What do you think, Jake? Do you think Amy was pushed?" They both stared at Jake, not an ounce of emotion showing in their expressions.

"Pushed?"

"That's what your mother claimed at the time," Detective Cameron replied evenly. "Said Amy probably knew her killer too."

Jake fought the anger rising inside him. He could sense where their accusations were heading and knew any irritation on his part would only act to fuel their ideas.

"I have never questioned that Amy's death was anything other than a result of her fall from the rocks. I can still remember, as clear as day, the trauma my mum went through and I didn't pay heed to what she said then or since. Now, of course, I can see it's a coincidence that my sister's body was discovered in the same place as this girl's but I don't see how you can imagine I'm involved in any way."

"But don't you see, Jake?" Detective Cameron leaned forward eagerly. "You are a connection! You were in the woods, exactly where we've found the body of our missing girl, which is also where your sister's body was discovered. You were Amy's brother; she would have trusted you up there on the hilltop with her. Maybe it was a childish game which went too far and you pushed her over the edge? You'd have panicked, of course. Probably ran home and pretended none of it happened whilst poor old Amy, fatally injured, dragged herself as far as she could in search of help."

Jake simply looked at him. Then glanced at the other man's steely stare. They had to be mad; no way could they actually believe any of this, Jake thought. But their eyes remained fixed on him, no doubt gauging his reaction and the time it was taking him to respond to their crazy theory. His brain bumbled through a string of things to say as he opened and closed his mouth helplessly.

"Do I need a solicitor?" Jake asked.

"You tell me, Jake, do you?"

Jake shook his head slowly. "No, I bloody well don't, and you know it. This is ridiculous. You're saying I killed my sister when I was ten! Why? And I didn't even know this girl. You should be out there looking for the real killer, not dragging innocent people in off the street who were in the wrong place at the wrong time." Pausing, Jake felt his chest heaving, but at least he felt better for his little outburst.

Detective Cameron was shuffling some papers in a folder on the desk in front of him. Eventually, he closed the folder and looked back at Jake, smiling.

"Okay, Jake, I'm happy to let you go, for now, but I want you to remain at the B&B, just in case we have any further questions for you. Thank you for your co-operation today."

Jake tried to hide his surprise and relief. He'd had visions of spending the night in a dark police cell.

Refusing the offer of a lift back to the village, Jake stood outside the police station. Legs feeling slightly wobbly, he headed into the city centre. He found a quiet café, ordered a coffee and looked at his mobile.

It was no good, Jake thought, he was going to have to phone his mum. If he didn't go home when he'd said, she'd worry; she was going to worry now, whatever he did, but at least she'd have time to calm down before he saw her again.

Just as he'd expected: she'd lurched from crying to angry accusations and back again countless times during the phone call. Even threatening to get the first train to Sheffield, Jake hoped he'd managed to calm her down sufficiently; he didn't need a hysterical mother coming down here and embarrassing him in front of the police.

Returning to Bradfield after dark, Jake found the B&B in darkness. He'd expected his landlady to be waiting with a string of questions ready, instead, as he opened the door to his room, he stooped to pick up the folded note which had been pushed under the door.

She wanted him to vacate his room, wasn't prepared to have her reputation, or that of her establishment, tarnished with regular visits from the local constabulary.

Jake couldn't help but smile to himself as he dropped onto his bed. One visit to help them with their enquiries and suddenly he'd been branded as a hardened criminal. No doubt, every person in the two villages knew he'd been taken to the police station now, thanks to her misplaced sense of civic duty

Richard was sympathetic to Jake's dilemma but there wasn't a spare bedroom at his parents' place. Jokingly, he'd suggested Jake ask Martha, and as much as it created some unease inside him, Jake didn't see that he had any other option. Bradfield was hardly a thriving metropolis with hotels around every corner. The police had begrudgingly accepted he was leaving the B&B, but insisted he remain in the local vicinity and keep in touch with them as to his whereabouts.

Already filled with a sense of unjustified guilt, Jake made his way up to Martha's bungalow, trying not to pre-empt the reception he'd receive.

As before, the place seemed deserted and his knock at the front door gained no response from inside. Thinking he could faintly hear music from inside, Jake walked round to the gate and went into the backyard.

The back door was closed. Jake knocked again and waited. About to give up and turn away, Jake saw Martha peer at him from the shadows in the hallway, across the far side of the kitchen.

He smiled and gave her a small wave. After a moment's hesitation, Martha came to the door and slowly pulled it open.

She looked tired, he thought. Her face was pale but the skin beneath her eyes was dark. Her hair was drawn back from her face, loosely held by a ribbon. Small, bare feet showed below the hem of her long, flowered skirt and the white, cotton shirt she wore, was thin, showing she wore nothing beneath it.

Her appearance of innocence and natural beauty created an instant reaction in Jake which he fought to hide, wishing to make a favourable, friendly impression.

"Hi Martha; can I come in?" He thought she blushed slightly, but after only a brief pause, Martha stepped back and Jake took it as an invitation to enter.

As soon as she closed the door, Jake turned to her: "I'm really sorry if I upset you the other day; it was entirely unintentional."

Receiving no reply, he hurried on: "I don't know what I did, or said, wrong, but I want you to know, I never meant to hurt you. You're my oldest friend and I don't want to lose you over some misunderstanding."

Still with no response, Jake searched his head for something further to add. Then, as he looked at her face, Jake saw she was smiling. "You enjoying this?" he asked hopefully. "Seeing me squirm?"

Then she giggled, a tuneful, child-like giggle. Immediately Jake felt himself cast back into the school playground facing the younger Martha as she laughed at his reaction to her teasing him.

"We okay then?"

She nodded, still smiling at him.

"Do you want to tell me how I upset you, so I can avoid making the same mistake?"

"No," she replied curtly. "Tea?"

"No, thanks," Jake replied. "I need to ask a favour."

As Martha just looked at him, Jake continued: "I need to check out of my B&B. I was wondering whether I could kip on your floor, just for a few days."

Frowning as she watched him, Martha put the kettle down. "Has something happened?"

"It's stupid!" Jake replied, flinging his arms into the air. "They've found that missing girl's body. The police wanted to ask me some questions and now my landlady seems to think I'm some sort of child-killer. She wants me to move out but the police want me to remain in the area. I need somewhere to stay." He looked at her apologetically. "I couldn't think of anyone else to ask."

Briefly, Jake thought she was about to rebuke his request. But, after a short pause, her smile returned.

"Why did the police want to question you?" Martha asked.

Jake shrugged. "Someone saw me in the woods and thought I looked suspicious. Can't blame them!" he added playfully.

Martha watched him. "Are you sure you're not toying with me? There's no ulterior motive in all this?"

Jake shook his head. He thought his request was simple. "I'm sorry, Martha," he admitted, "you've lost me again."

Martha took a deep breath, looking at him as if he was a child. "Very well, but the floor is all I can offer you."

"That's fine, it's great," Jake replied quickly before she could change her mind. "You're a life-saver."

"Now then," Martha began, picking up the kettle again and holding it beneath the tap. "Would you like some tea?"

Jake hesitated. "Would you mind if I went and got my stuff from the B&B? I think the landlady will feel much happier once I'm completely gone. I must admit, I'd rather get it over and done with; I know when I'm not wanted."

"Fine, you go and I'll make some space," Martha replied.

"Don't go to any trouble," Jake stated. "I don't have much, just a holdall and rucksack."

Nodding as she disappeared into the hallway, Jake smiled to himself as he let himself out of the house, once again totally confused by his feelings for this woman. Richard had been right: she was weird.

When Jake checked out of the B&B, it was the least talkative his landlady had ever been. She was curt but polite, clearly finding great effort in holding back what she wanted to say to him. Stepping back onto the street, Jake breathed a sigh of relief. Having informed the police where he would be staying, he headed back up the hill to Martha's bungalow.

As usual the place was silent and to save time, Jake simply went straight to the back door and let himself in, calling out her name as he closed the door behind him.

Following the sound of music into the sitting room, Jake gave a gentle knock on the door before entering the room.

Martha smiled up at him from her position on the sofa. Her legs curled up beneath her body, she held a book open on her lap.

"Where would you like me to put this?" Jake asked, holding up his bags.

Martha jumped up. "Follow me," she told him and led him back into the hallway where he followed her to a door at the end of the corridor.

She led him into a bedroom; it was small and bare. A pair of orange curtains were closed across the window. She'd evidently made him up a make-shift bed on the floor which seemed to consist of a deep pile of blankets and covers with a pair of plump pillows at one end. The carpet was filled with purple swirls, the painted walls were lilac and a single light bulb hung from a fitting in the centre of the ceiling.

Jake dropped his bags by the bed and rubbed his hands together, fixing a smile on his lips. "It looks great, Martha, thanks a lot, I really appreciate this."

She seemed relieved by his reaction to the room and visibly relaxed. "Should I make us some tea?"

"Yeah, that'll be great," he reassured her. "I'll just sort my stuff out and then I'll be through."

Martha disappeared and as Jake took his things out of his bags, trying to make the room look a little less stark, he heard Martha pottering in the kitchen, quietly singing to herself.

Having unpacked, Jake peeked through the curtains. His room looked out into the back yard. He pulled the curtains closed again and went into the sitting room.

Martha was back on the sofa, this time pouring some tea into two cups. A plate of biscuits sat on the coffee table. Jake helped himself to a digestive before he sat on the armchair.

"Don't you have a TV?" he asked, looking around the room.

"No, sorry," she apologised. "I've never bothered."

She placed his cup in front of him and returned to her own place. Strains of a big band tune crackled from the gramophone as Jake sipped his tea and nibbled at his biscuit. He was aware of Martha gazing back at the pages of her book, periodically casting a glance in his direction.

"You're welcome to choose something for yourself," she suggested, indicating one of the bookshelves.

Jake glanced down at his mobile. There was no phone signal and he didn't imagine for one moment Martha had wifi, he hadn't seen any evidence of a telephone even.

Squinting at the titles along the book spines, Jake thumbed a couple of books. He'd not read a book since school, and that had been under pressure. Settling for an anthology of poems, he sat back down as Martha changed the record.

Part of him admired her for her independence and refusal to conform to the twenty first century, he knew he couldn't do it, he liked his creature comforts too much and enjoyed company. There was no way he could imagine himself existing in such a lonely location as this.

After two more biscuits and skimming his eyes over a couple of poems, Jake made a great performance of yawning and stretching his arms. "I'm going to hit the sack," he told her.

Martha smiled. "Good idea, I won't be much longer myself."

"Night, then," Jake said as he stood up, leaving the book on the table.

"Night," Martha replied. "You can take it with you, if you want."

"Thanks," he replied, picking the paperback up and clutching it to his chest.

Hurriedly, Jake cleaned his teeth and used the loo in the bathroom, before closing his bedroom door. Surveying the room, he realised there was no way he could reach the light switch from moving his bed into any position. He stripped down to his boxer shorts, extinguished the light and quickly got under the covers. Twisting himself until he found a reasonably comfortable position, Jake closed his eyes, listening for the sounds of the building. He was used to noise. Even at the B&B there had been sounds of traffic, voices and the occasional owl. Here, there was nothing; the silence was unnerving. It wasn't until the hall light was extinguished and his room fell into total darkness, that Jake realised he'd been holding his body tense.

Forcing himself to relax, he tried to focus on his breathing, ignoring the voice inside his head, reminding him that he and Martha were the only two people in the place.

She stood in the open bedroom doorway. The only light shone from the hallway behind her. Despite the presence of her long nightdress, it was evident she was naked beneath it.

Jake blinked and swept his hand across his eyes. He was helpless, mesmerised by the sight of her. As he watched Martha, her hands loosened the ties at the neck of her nightdress and it fell to the floor. Her hour-glass figure was more perfect than he'd imagined. Silently, she stepped forward until she stood by his bed. The noise of his thumping heart was the only sound in the room as Martha knelt and drew back the covers from his body.

Feeling her eyes on his erection, Jake held his breath as she moved slowly towards him and then felt her lips on his. Her hand gently began to caress his cock as she slid silently into his bed.

He woke with a start. Immediately Jake remembered what had occurred in the night. His bedding was in disarray but he was alone. Had he imagined it? Had Martha really come into his room? Drawing his covers around him, Jake was embarrassed by his memories. It had been so real, yet now, he doubted his own mind. How was he going to face her? he wondered, whether it had been real or not?

Pressure on his bladder eventually drove Jake from his room. Pulling a T-shirt over his head, he padded down the hall to the bathroom. He realised the room was full of steam as soon as he pushed the door open.

Martha looked at him from the bathtub, surrounded by bubbles.

Jake began blustering an apology.

She laughed. "Don't mind me," Martha chuckled.

"I'll just …" Jake backed towards the door.

"Don't be silly," Martha cried. "Do what you need to do; don't worry." She closed her eyes, leaning back and sliding lower into the water.

Embarrassed, but not wanting to appear shy, Jake turned his back towards her and relieved himself as quickly as he was able.

He washed his hands and splashed some cold water over his face, trying to act as though he was used to sharing a bathroom with a beautiful, young woman.

"Can you pass me the towel?" Martha was pointing towards a wooden chair which stood next to the toilet.

Jake reached for the towel and held it out towards Martha. She stood up as he turned back to the bath. He lowered his eyes quickly, although not before seeing her naked body standing, facing him.

"Sorry," he muttered.

"What for?" Martha asked, wrapping the towel around her body as she stepped out onto a rug.

"For blundering in here when you were in the bath."

Martha laughed. "I told you: don't be silly."

"You should have locked the door," Jake told her.

"There is no lock," she replied. "Anyway, why should I? Do I need to be scared of you, Jake?"

He looked at her and saw she was laughing at him. Martha wasn't embarrassed by his presence; it was almost as if she'd wanted him to see her nakedness. Jake knew, he was the only one who was uncomfortable with the situation. Without another word, he left the room, closed the door behind him and went back to his bedroom, sure he could hear her laughter.

He pulled on his clothes quickly. Then, checking the hall was clear, he went to the kitchen in search of some breakfast. At the sound of a noise behind him, Jake turned to see Martha watching him, now fully dressed.

"Don't you eat?" he asked her, pointing at the almost empty fridge.

She shrugged and picked up the kettle from the stove.

"I'll go down to the village and get some supplies," Jake told her.

Retrieving his jacket and wallet from his room, Jake then paused by the back door. He picked at an invisible spot on the door handle. He looked up and saw her watching him.

"Did anything happen last night?" he asked eventually, feeling the heat radiating from his face.

Martha frowned. "Happen? Like what?"

Jake watched her. There was no clue as to whether she knew what he was trying to say or whether she was teasing him, forever holding the upper hand.

"Nothing," he sighed and closed the door behind him.

Jake shoved his hands deep into his pockets. Martha would be the death of him, he decided. She was either a vixen, toying with him like a pet, or she really was the most innocent person he'd ever met.

He devoured a bacon roll ravenously. The coffee tasted like nectar after the insipid tea he'd felt obliged to drink at Martha's.

Cursing himself for not thinking of bringing his rucksack to carry his purchases back up the hill, Jake walked slowly, the handles of the carrier bags digging painfully into his fingers. Periodically, he stopped and readjusted the weighting of the bags.

There was no longer a fleet of police cars parked along the grass verge. Now, only a ribbon of cordons across the main entrance to the woods evidenced there had so recently been a battalion of officers in the village.

A group of teenagers occupied the swings in the children's play area next to the cricket ground. Smiling to himself, Jake recalled seeing the same sight repeatedly when he'd lived here as a child.

Sighing, Jake picked up his bags and continued up the hill.

As usual, it was the sound of the gramophone which greeted Jake as he opened the back door. Wearily, he lifted his shopping onto the kitchen counter and began unpacking his purchases.

Silently, Martha entered the room. Jake felt her hands slip over his eyes.

He smiled. "I know it's you, Martha."

She giggled and moved her hands from his face. He felt her arms wrap themselves around his waist. Her head rested against his back.

Jake stopped what he was doing. He was going to be a wreck before the police would ever let him leave this place, Jake decided. Every time Martha touched him, he could feel the effect of the physical contact inside him. She had no idea how far she was pushing his desire, or maybe she did and this was one big game to her.

Receiving no response, Martha released her hold on him and then began inspecting the items laid out on the worktop.

"You hungry?" Jake asked her.

Martha shook her head. "I've eaten," she told him, picking up the kettle and taking it to the sink. "Tea?"

Jake laughed. He turned to face her, sweeping his hand through his hair. "Is that all you do? Listen to music, read and drink tea?"

She looked hurt.

"Sorry," Jake said quickly. "None of my business what you do. I really am grateful to you for putting me up like this. Do you fancy going to the pub tonight? I'll buy you dinner."

"We'll see," Martha replied. She turned away and left Jake alone.

"Can I make you a sandwich?" he called after her. No reply came as he found a home for each of the things he'd bought.

With a couple of slices of buttered toast on a plate and a glass of orange juice, Jake went through to the sitting room. It was empty. He felt guilty for feeling relief that the gramophone was silent for a change. Jake hoped Martha wasn't annoyed with him; he didn't want to think of her hiding from him in her own home.

He ate his toast and drained his glass. Having cleared away, Jake knocked gently on Martha's bedroom door. "You okay in there?"

"Come in," Martha called.

Relieved she'd responded to him, Jake pushed the door open.

Everywhere appeared pink: the walls, curtains, light shade and bedding. A chair in the corner was smothered in cuddly toys and a fluffy, pink rug sat next to the bed. Martha was sitting crossed-legged on the single divan, a book in her hand.

She looked at him as though eager for a response. "What do you think?" she prompted him.

"Think?" Jake scratched his scalp.

"My room?"

Taken aback, Jake smiled. "It's, it's very pink?"

Martha laughed. "A bit much?"

"Maybe? Unless you like pink," Jake suggested.

"And you don't?"

"Not really my colour," he replied.

Martha patted the patchwork quilt in front of her.

Jake crossed the short distance from the door to the bed and perched on the edge. "You okay?"

Martha nodded. She laid her book down and picked up his hand in hers. She brushed her lips against the back of his hand.

Jake watched her face, wanting some clue as to what she expected from him. He didn't want to take advantage of her inviting him into her home, neither did he want her to think he wasn't attracted to her. He shifted his position, pulling his leg up beneath him so he could see her better.

"You are beautiful," he risked.

Martha looked at him. Her eyes sparkled as a faint pink lit her cheeks. Their fingers lay intertwined between them.

Jake stopped searching for things to say, suddenly he realised no words were necessary. The silence was comfortable and he felt himself beginning to relax.

Leaning forward slightly, Jake gently kissed her lips. His fingers rested against her hair; it was even silkier than he'd imagined. As she began to kiss him back, Jake moved his body closer to hers.

Pulling back to look at her, Jake's fingers traced a line round her face. He shook himself slightly, "I've got to ask you again," he began, "did anything happen between us last night?"

"Like what?" she replied huskily, moving her lips back towards his.

One moment they were kissing, Jake, receiving no objection, allowing his hands to slowly explore the contours of Martha's petite frame; then suddenly, she drew her head back, looked down at her clothing and began smoothing out the creases.

She cleared her throat and stood up unsteadily. "Shall I make us some tea?" With the absence of a response, Martha hurried from the room.

Jake let out a huge sigh. What was her game? He waited until the fire inside him became subdued. Looking around her bedroom, Jake realised how much it appeared like that belonging to a child. He wondered how much, if at all, it had changed since Martha's childhood. Suddenly he knew the mood had gone and he was desperate to get out of the house.

With his jacket in his hand, Jake went through to the kitchen. Martha was preparing the tea tray.

"I need to pop out," he told her. "I've got a couple of calls I promised to make. Shall I come back for you later so we can go to the pub?"

It looked like she was about to rebuke him, then, her face softened and Martha nodded: "That'll be nice."

Jake gave her a small smile before stepping outside.

He had no one in particular to see. He'd have a look and see if Richard was around, but the day loomed ahead of him so Jake's pace was slow as he descended towards the village.

Stepping onto the grass verge as the sound of a vehicle came towards him, Jake was surprised when the blue mini halted next to him. He peered down through the open passenger window and saw Richard in the driver's seat.

"Where've you been?"

"Hiya," Jake returned. "I'm staying at Martha's place. I was hoping to bump into you today."

"I'm just heading into Sheffield," Richard told him. "Fancy a pint later?"

"Yeah, I was going down there anyway; I'll see you then."

The car pulled away from the kerb and disappeared. Jake smiled, feeling less glum. Even the brief sighting of his old friend had helped to buoy his spirits. Jake wasn't sure whether it was Martha or her home which dragged him down. He couldn't put his finger on it, but there was something disturbing about her and her situation. Maybe she did spend too much time alone, wrapped up in her own isolated world. Some company down the pub might help to ease the pressure he felt: torn between wanting to be with Martha and seeing whether she was interested in him too, and the unnerving sense of fear he also experienced when in her presence. It was impossible to say exactly what made Jake feel uneasy but escaping from that bungalow, which seemed trapped in time, was always a relief.

The day passed surprisingly quickly. Jake knew he wanted to bathe or shower before they went to the pub so headed home with plenty of time to spare.

Martha appeared pleased to see him, running up to him as soon as he entered the kitchen and kissing him on the lips. She stepped back and gave a twirl; the long dark green dress swung out, revealing bare calves. The front was low-cut showing the rise of her pale, round breasts.

Jake forced his eyes to her face. She was smiling at him, clearly waiting for a response as to her appearance. Her long, dark hair hung loosely, dropping below her shoulders; her rose lips were slightly parted and her round, brown eyes looked at him from beneath long, dark lashes.

Ignoring the racing blood inside his body and the ache in his balls, Jake smiled and gave a brief: "You look lovely."

He could see she was hurt by his curt observation but continued: "Do you mind if I take a quick shower before we go?"

Glad the water was only lukewarm, Jake allowed it to extinguish the flames of his desire for Martha. He knew she must be toying with him. No woman could be unaware of that much sexual desire flying between them. She was a tease, he decided. Well, he was determined to regain and retain the upper hand. If she thought she could play with him, Jake was going to do his best to turn the tables on her. His physical desire for her was driving him mad but he would fight against it until Martha was begging him to come to her bed. He wouldn't be rude or ignore her, but he would do his best to resist her come-ons to put their relationship on a more even footing.

Jake hoped the effect was satisfactory. It was difficult with so few of his things with him but his trousers looked smart, the open-necked shirt was crease-free and his hair, slightly wavy and slicked back, always looked best just out of the shower. He hoped the after-shave was subtle enough. He'd not bothered to shave, a couple of days stubble helped him look slightly older and Jake hoped Martha liked the rugged appearance.

Her eyes seemed to devour him as he stepped into the kitchen. Jake smiled inwardly and took the liberty of awarding himself a silent point.

"Shall we go?" he asked quickly, opening the back door, and not giving her a chance to kiss him.

They strolled down the road, hand in hand. It was almost dark but it was a short walk downhill, with lights from the village showing their destination.

Inside the pub, the atmosphere was warm and welcoming. A buzz of voices greeted the newcomers as the door closed against the night. The place was busy but they found a table in a corner, Martha sat down whilst Jake went to the bar to order drinks.

He'd been irritated to learn she'd apparently eaten earlier. Jake assumed they'd agreed to eat together in the pub so he wasn't going to forego his dinner just to be polite; she'd have to watch him whilst he ate.

Having ordered his own meal, Jake carried their drinks to the table. He was taken aback by how unsure of herself Martha appeared in this environment. It was unlikely she visited a pub on her own but it was the first time he could recall seeing her uncomfortably adrift.

Jake kept the conversation light, trying to put her at her ease. Her self-consciousness added to her appeal, as far as he was concerned, making Jake feel protective towards her.

A sudden slap on his back as he took a gulp from his pint, had Jake spluttering as he tried to prevent himself from dribbling onto his shirt.

"Sorry, mate," Richard said, as he dropped into an empty chair, placing his pint on their table.

The two men shook hands. Jake nodded towards Martha. "You remember Martha? Martha, this is Richard Taylor."

She smiled and lowered her eyes to her glass of orange juice.

Richard winked at Jake before launching into a stream of chatter.

Jake was glad of Richard's company. His friendly banter helped Jake forget about his concern for Martha. She seemed content to listen to their conversation, offering a smile whenever either of them glanced in her direction.

It was evident Richard was attracted to her too; his eyes repeatedly went to her face whenever he paused, slowly moving to the front of her dress before he dragged his attention back to Jake.

They chatted about other names from the past. Jake's burger and fries arrived at the table; Richard helped himself to a chip periodically, between anecdotes.

When he'd finished eating, Jake leaned back, his stomach satisfied. Richard placed another pint of beer in front of him, as he returned to the table.

Almost at once, Martha stood up. Both men looked at her.

"I'm going to head home," she told them.

Jake began to speak, torn between his two companions.

"No," Martha interrupted quickly. "I'm fine, really. You stay and catch up with Richard," she told Jake. "I'll see you later."

After the briefest of smiles at Richard, Martha disappeared out of the door.

Jake watched the closed door.

"What's she like then?" Richard interrupted his thoughts with a wide grin.

"Like?" Jake asked, returning his attention to Richard.

"You know," Richard smiled knowingly.

Jake chuckled. "How would I know?" He took a swig from his glass.

"You mean you haven't …"

Jake gazed at Richard. "No, we haven't."

"What! You're crazy!" Richard was shaking his head.

Jake shrugged. "I'm not going to push it, am I?"

"She's bloody gorgeous," Richard cried. "Little old Martha has certainly blossomed, who'd have thought it?" His eyes glazed over and Jake tried to ignore what he knew Richard was imagining.

They sat quietly, each thinking only of Martha.

Eventually, Richard broke the silence. "I'm glad I bumped into you earlier," he began enthusiastically. "I've got an interview to do tomorrow and I wondered whether you might be interested in joining me."

Jake frowned.

"I'm trying to put a piece together about the girl's murder," Richard said, nodding his head towards the woods. "Turns out the old vicar was a bit of an expert on local legend. Someone suggested I speak to him. I thought, with what happened to your sister, you might like to come along and hear what he has to say."

"The old vicar?" Jake asked.

"Yeah, he was here when we were kids, but lives in a retirement home on the edge of the city now. I talked to a member of their staff and they said he'd be happy to chat to me."

Jake pulled a face. It felt weird, after the years of hearing his mum's strange ideas about Amy's death. On the other hand, he knew it was tough filling his days here whilst he was obliged to remain in the area.

"Yeah, why not?" he replied eventually.

The conversation returned to the mundane as they chatted and drank until closing time. By the time they stepped outside, the shock of the cold air was like a bucket of icy water on Jake.

They exchanged 'goodbyes' with Richard saying he would pick Jake up outside Martha's at eleven the following morning.

As he walked up the road, Jake tried to ignore the nausea in his stomach and let his eyes relax to avoid the double-vision he was experiencing. He couldn't recall the last time he'd spent an entire evening in a pub drinking. At twenty, he knew he should be a little better prepared for the after-effects.

The bungalow was in darkness. Trying to be as quiet as he could, Jake paused briefly outside Martha's bedroom door. All was silent. As an image of her lying naked, waiting for him, came into his head, Jake hurried to his own room and quietly closed the door.

She'd come to his bed noiselessly, waking him with her eager hands on his torso. Before he could say anything, her mouth was on his. He felt her nakedness against his own skin and thought he would explode with desire.

Only his sleepy and drunken grogginess held Jake back as Martha took control of their love-making. Feeling her hand on his hard cock as she guided him towards her open legs, Jake opened his eyes wanting to see her face.

He pushed himself back in horror, only half-suppressing the scream which came from his mouth, sounding alien to his own ears.

He was panting breathlessly as he looked at the old, lined face before him; it looked like Martha but with an extra thirty or forty years added. The woman grinned before moving towards him again, her sagging breasts rocking heavily as she crept forwards.

"No," Jake cried and leapt out of bed much more quickly than he would have considered himself capable of.

The room was suddenly bathed in light as the door opened and Martha stood in the doorway looking at him.

Jake glanced from his empty bed, then back at Martha. Quickly he was aware of his nakedness and that, her expression had altered from one of concern to quiet amusement.

He put his hands in front of his now semi-limp cock and muttered an incomprehensible apology for waking her.

"Night," Martha called as she closed the door behind her.

Jake stood still, his body shaking slightly from the nightmare and the chilliness of the room. As he lowered himself back onto his bed, leaving the light on, he was mystified at the reality of his dream. She had appeared so real; he had felt her skin on his own and his cock had evidently decided she was in his bed. He thumped his fist to his forehead. He wasn't making much of a success at being the one in charge of their relationship.

Groaning at the realisation there was daylight now forcing its way through the curtains, Jake forced his eyes to open. He blinked repeatedly, adjusting his sight to the new day. Wanting nothing other than the opportunity to turn over and go back to sleep, Jake cursed himself for agreeing to go out with Richard. He couldn't phone him and make his excuses because of the lack of mobile coverage, and it would be too rude to let Richard turn up on the doorstep and then announce he wouldn't be going.

Begrudgingly, Jake dragged himself out of bed and into the shower. He felt inexplicably angry. The crooning of a long-dead jazz singer, coming from the direction of the sitting room added to Jake's irritation. Once again, the temperature of the water could hardly be defined as hot and he knew if he walked into the kitchen and Martha offered him a cup of blasted tea, he was likely to say something he'd regret. Resolving to pay a visit to the police after seeing Richard and the vicar, Jake hoped he could convince them he wasn't about to skip the country and persuade them to allow him to return home and to work. He was sure there would be some way in which he could liaise with his local constabulary to keep Detective Cameron content.

Surprised to find the kitchen empty, rather than searching Martha out, Jake scribbled her a note to explain he would be out all day and left the house before she could appear.

Annoyed to see Richard looking more animated than he felt himself, Jake slid into the passenger seat as the car moved off from the kerb again.

Feeling the hairs stand on the back of his neck, Jake turned back to glance at the bungalow. For an instant, he thought he saw Martha standing in the driveway, looking as she had when they'd been at school together; he shivered. There was no one.

"You look rough," Richard reassured him with a smile.

Jake grunted his reply and looked out of his window at the passing countryside.

"Martha too hot for you to handle?" Richard persisted.

"Give it a rest," Jake told him.

Richard roared with laughter, clearly thinking his assumption was correct, rather than that Jake was feeling sorry for himself and suffering the ill-effects of too much beer.

They continued the journey in silence. Jake lost his bearings once they reached the city and gazed unseeingly at the numerous turnings and buildings until the car turned into a driveway flanked by tall, green hedges.

The gravelled driveway wound downhill, bordered by vast lawns dotted with mature trees. Eventually a large stone, square house came into view and Richard parked in a bay marked for visitors.

"Not bad?" Richard suggested, pointing at the view whilst reaching onto the backseat for a small rucksack.

Jake pulled himself out of the car and looked in the direction his friend had indicated. The city was spread out before them, hills dispersed in every direction so that Sheffield looked like a stage in an amphitheatre.

Jake smiled and nodded before following Richard into the porch of the house.

"Leave the talking to me," Richard told him as they crossed a wood-panelled hallway towards a reception desk.

A wide, carpeted staircase wound round two walls of the hall, a stair-lift sat idle at the foot. From behind the wide desk, adorned with computer and blotting pad, a middle-aged woman beamed a welcoming smile.

Jake looked round the room whilst Richard spoke to the receptionist. It had evidently been a very grand home, once upon a time; dark portraits rubbed shoulders with framed certificates and a red fire extinguisher rested next to a grubby dinner gong.

At one end, a large archway opened into a lounge; Jake could see an array of high-backed armchairs irregularly placed, but all facing towards a large television screen. At the opposite end of the hall, a long, brightly-lit corridor led into the bowels of the building. It all seemed very calm and quiet; Jake decided there would be worse places to live out one's existence.

They were led by a sullen orderly up the stairs and along a corridor which seemed to mirror the one Jake had noticed downstairs. The doors lining the corridor were identical except for the brass numbers attached to each one.

They stopped at number seven. The orderly gave a brief knock, told them to wait and disappeared into the room.

"Don't think I'd want him looking after me," Jake commented with a grin, relieved to be starting to feel human again.

Richard chuckled as he stepped from one foot to the other as they waited.

The orderly reappeared, told them not to let his patient become too over-excited and to let him know if they needed anything, before he walked back along the corridor.

Richard knocked on the door and walked into the room. Jake followed and closed the door. He was surprised by the small size of the room, having expected something much grander after the other parts of the house he'd seen.

Apart from the dark, antique wardrobe in the corner of the room, and the grey carpet on the floor, it was like any hospital room with a large, adjustable bed, angle-poised lamp and bedside table filling the centre of the room. A high-back, wipe-clean chair stood on either side of the bed and, as Richard took a seat on the far side of the bed, Jake sat in the one closest to him before turning his attention to the occupant of the bed.

The man looked shrivelled lying in the huge bed. His hair was thick but white and he looked lost inside a quilted blue dressing gown. Despite his small demeanour, he was clearly alert as he took in both his visitors quickly.

Jake listened as Richard explained the reason for their visit after introducing himself and then Jake.

Reverend Jackson's eyes lingered on Jake. "You're the boy whose sister died so tragically." His voice rang clear and unexpectedly deep.

Jake nodded. "Yes, Amy, she died ten years ago. I'm sorry, I don't really remember you, I was only young," he explained.

Reverend Jackson held up his hand. "Don't worry, I'm not offended," he said with a chuckle. He turned his attention back to Richard. "Now, young man, what is it you would like to know?"

"I understand, when you were in High Bradfield, you were the expert on local stories and legends," Richard began. "You've, no doubt, heard that the missing girl's body was found in the woods, in the same place the police discovered Jake's sister's corpse." He cast a look of apology in Jake's direction but continued. "I wondered, with your knowledge, whether you thought there might be more than just a coincidence that both girls were discovered in the woods."

Both young men watched the old man as his eyes closed. Jake glanced at Richard, wondering if he was sleeping or bored by their company. Richard shrugged and turned his attention back to the priest, clearing his throat.

The old man's eyes opened at once. He looked at Richard before turning his attention to Jake. "What do you think happened to your sister?" he asked.

Jake couldn't hide his surprise at the question. "She fell from the hilltop," he replied, unsure whether the old man recalled the details of Amy's death. "The police believe she dragged herself as far as the woods but died of her injuries before she was discovered."

"Oh, never mind what the police believe," Reverend Jackson blurted, waving his hand dismissively. "What about you, and your mum? What do you think happened?"

Jake realised they were both looking at him now and he squirmed in his chair. "I don't have any reason not to believe them," he muttered defensively.

"Poppycock!" The old man exclaimed. "Although, I suppose you were only a child at the time," he added, as though to make allowance for Jake's ignorance.

"What do you think happened to Amy?" Richard asked, drawing his chair forward, notepad balanced on his lap and biro raised in mid-air.

"Me?" Reverend Jackson cried. "What do I know? I'm a man of God; no time to spare for speculation and superstition."

Jake thought the old man winked at him, but he couldn't be sure. It was hard to tell whether he was simply enjoying some company or actually had any theories on the deaths.

"Okay," Richard said, resting his notepad on the bed, "if you weren't a vicar and knew two girls had been found dead in those woods, would you think it was a coincidence or – something more sinister?"

Jake watched Richard lean back in his chair. He looked triumphant.

Jake wondered what his mum would think if she could see him now. Would she be relieved to see him, apparently, engaging in ideas about Amy's death not having been accidental?

Reverend Jackson stared at Richard. Again, he addressed his speech towards Jake. "There is something evil in those woods; it's been there for centuries. Why they ever let people roam in there is beyond me." His eyes glazed over as he appeared to slip into a daze.

Jake realised Richard was grinning in his direction; he was certainly doing a good job of looking like a journalist on the verge of a breakthrough with a decent story.

"Can you explain what you mean?" Richard prompted, after the old man had remained silent for a couple of minutes.

He seemed to suddenly recall their presence and pulled himself further up in his bed. "You know there was once a castle on Bailey Hill?"

Richard nodded.

"There was a cruel execution there, a woman robbed too soon of her life." He began coughing.

Richard filled the plastic cup on the table from a jug of water and held it out but the old man's face was becoming crimson.

"I'll go and get help," Jake cried, jumping out of his seat and heading for the door.

They were both ushered from the room as several members of staff descended. Loitering in the corridor for what seemed ages, eventually they were told Reverend Jackson was sedated and wouldn't be up to visitors any more that day.

Dejectedly, Richard led the way back to his car. "Bloody hell!" he cried as he put the key in the ignition and slammed his hand against the steering wheel.

"We could go to the library," Jake suggested. "We're bound to find something out now we have a place to begin."

Richard seemed to consider the idea. He glanced at his watch. "I've got to head into the office; can I drop you off on the bus route? We can meet in the pub later and decide what to do?"

"Or I could go to the library for you?" Jake asked.

"No," Richard replied quickly. "let's leave it for now. It would be better if we can speak to the old guy again, maybe tomorrow, and then back up what he tells us with some research afterwards."

Jake didn't argue. It was Richard's call and he wasn't sure he wanted to discover some malevolent cause behind his sister's death anyway.

Stepping off the bus back in Bradfield, Jake paused. The sun was shining but the air was chilly. He felt loathe to walk up the hill and face Martha at present and the desire to go for a walk had been taken away by the accusations from the police. In the end, he headed to the café at the Schoolrooms; they served great coffee and he realised he'd eaten nothing all day.

Later, feeling contented, as he walked through High Bradfield on his way back to Martha's, Jake thought he recognised a voice near the pub.

"Mum?" Jake cried. He stared in disbelief at his mother standing on the pavement with Pasquale, seemingly in the middle of a heated disagreement. Both paused at the sound of Jake's voice and turned to stare at him.

"What are you two doing here?" he asked, walking towards them.

"We were looking for you," Marion explained, as she wrapped her arms round his neck and kissed his cheek.

"Why? What's happened?" Jake asked, looking from one of them to the other.

"What's happened?" Marion repeated. "You! You're what's happened. Did you really think you could phone me like you did from the police station and then not even pick up the phone once to say you were okay? I've been worried sick, Jacob Brooks."

"What about you?" Jake threw his question at Pasquale who was leaning against the bonnet of his white MG.

"Your poor mother had been phoning me non-stop. The least I could do was offer to drive her here to see if we could find you," he explained.

Jake cringed. He could just imagine Pasquale trying desperately to calm his mother on the phone whilst running his kitchen at the same time; his name must have been dragged through the mud a few times.

"I'm sorry," Jake cried, hugging his mum and looking apologetically at his friend. "The phone reception is rubbish here."

"I thought you were staying at this B&B," his mum said, pulling herself away from him and pointing at the building they were standing by.

"I was, until the landlady decided I was bad news and kicked me out."

"So, where have you been sleeping?" Marion asked.

Jake looked at her. He knew she was going to flip. "Martha's."

Marion turned away from him as soon as the name was mentioned.

Pasquale looked at her downcast head, then turned to Jake. "Who's Martha?"

Jake opened his mouth to respond but his mum was quicker.

"Martha is a nasty little bitch who murdered my daughter and then got her claws well and truly stuck into my son!" Although speaking to Pasquale, Marion stared at her son, angry at his admission, yet not wholly surprised.

"You can't say that, Mum," Jake said quietly.

"I will say whatever I please as far as that cow is concerned."

Pasquale was embarrassed. He'd thought he'd been doing the right thing by helping Marion out and bringing her here, now he wasn't so sure.

"You don't have to like her," Jake began.

Marion snorted in disbelief.

"But she's been kind, took me in when I had nowhere else to stay. What did you expect me to do? Doss down in the churchyard?"

Marion stopped herself saying the rebuff which sat on her tongue. Anything would have been better than having her son at the beck and call of that evil child. She shuddered as their previous encounters came into her head. It seemed they had come back at the right time, she decided.

"Well, you can get your things and leave with us," Marion told Jake.

"I can't," he replied. "The police won't let me go yet, in case they have any further questions for me."

"I'll see about that," Marion told him. "You can collect your things and then Pasquale can drive us to the police station."

Jake cringed at the thought of standing by his mother whilst she chastised Detective Cameron for not believing in her son's innocence.

"I can handle it, Mum. Why don't you let Pasquale drive you home and I'll make a point each day of finding some coverage so I can call you?"

Pasquale stood up, looking hopeful.

"I'm not leaving you with *her*," Marion spat.

Pasquale leant back against his car.

"Come with me then and see Martha," Jake said. "She's changed, Mum; we all have. Martha's a young woman now; you don't need to worry about me. I can look after myself, you know?"

Marion looked at her son. She knew he was old enough to look after himself. Amy had been vulnerable and Martha had taken advantage of that. Jake was a man but he would always be her little boy, her only child now; she felt an overwhelming urge to protect him. If Martha was a woman, it only meant she had more capacity for evil, as far as Marion was concerned.

"Show me where she lives," she said quietly.

"She still lives up at the same bungalow she lived in as a child," Jake replied.

They climbed into Pasquale's car and Jake directed him the short distance up to Martha's home.

Marion stared out of the car window. It felt like a knife was slowly cutting around her heart as she gazed out at the old, familiar sights. She'd never imagined coming back to this place and she didn't want to lose her son here either.

Pasquale said he'd stay in the car as he pulled into the driveway. Marion stared at the bungalow as she waited for Jake to climb out of the back of the car. It seemed a lifetime ago since she'd been here, trying to discover what Martha could tell her about her dead daughter.

"Please don't be rude," Jake begged as he led his mum to the back door. Pausing, with his fingers on the door handle, despite his look of entreaty, his mother simply stared ahead of her, arms folded across her chest.

With a sigh, Jake pushed the door open.

Martha was standing by the sink. Her eyes moved from Jake, then quickly to Marion.

The two women stared at each other, silently eyeing the other. Jake felt as though he was in a room with a pair of hungry tigers.

Then, as quickly, the moment passed. "Tea?" Martha asked breezily.

Jake mumbled a 'yes', feeling quite sick and wishing he'd never invited his mum to come here.

"Hello Martha," Marion replied mechanically. "Tea would be lovely."

Martha hummed to herself as she pottered about the kitchen making preparations. Marion remained still, her eyes not leaving the face of the younger woman. Either Martha was a brilliant actress, Jake decided, or she was totally untouched by his mum's presence.

At last, with a laden tray in her hands, Martha beamed at Marion: "Please, follow me. Can you get the door?" she called to Jake.

He stood aside, holding the door open as Martha led the way to the living room.

As Martha came to a halt in front of the sofa, Marion moved across to the armchair so Jake was forced to take a seat on the sofa next to Martha.

Having poured three teas, Martha sat next to Jake. Fully aware that her thigh was against his own, he felt his face redden as she rested her hand on his leg.

It was evident his mum noted the action too. With a look of horror, she looked at his face.

Jake knew his smile was pathetic. Now his mum must be assuming he and Martha were an item.

"This is lovely," Martha said smiling, looking from Jake and back to Marion. "It was a wonderful surprise when Jake knocked on my door, out of the blue. And now we're living here together." She leaned against him, her hand travelling up his leg playfully as she squeezed his thigh.

"I'm sure it was," Marion snapped.

Jake tried to put a little distance between himself and Martha, but she moved along the sofa with him. "I do love him," she said, turning back to Marion. "We love each other."

Marion stood up. "This is ridiculous," she snapped. "Get your things, Jake, we're leaving."

"I can't," Jake replied, taking Martha's hand from his leg and dropping it into her own lap.

He stood up and faced his mother. "I know you don't like each other but I can't leave, not yet. Martha's a good friend; I need to be here. I can't just walk out."

Jake saw his mother glance down at Martha.

"You don't need to be embarrassed, Jake," Martha interrupted. "You know we're more than just friends."

His fingers clenched into fists. "Martha! Mum! What is going on? Why can't you both just be civil?"

Marion fought against the tears which threatened to fall. The image in her head of her son in bed with this person made her want to throw up.

"Are you coming with me or not?" Marion asked Jake.

He looked from his mum to Martha who was still seated, her hand gently rubbing his leg.

"I can't," Jake groaned.

Marion stood in front of her son, looking up at his face, ignoring the woman by his side. "I sincerely hope you don't regret this, Jake," she said. "If you aren't home in three days I will be back. And next time, I won't be leaving without you."

She glanced down at Martha. "You are poison. If you do anything to harm my son, I will come after you," she warned. With that, Marion pushed past Jake. They heard the sound of the back-door slamming shut. A moment later a car engine roared into life before it faded into the distance.

"I'm sorry," Jake began shakily. "I don't know why she's like that."

Martha took his hand and pulled him down onto the sofa beside her and Jake soon forgot about his mum's visit.

Chapter 6

It was intoxicating. His mum had been right; Martha was like a poison, but it was the sweetest and most potent kind he had ever imagined. She did things to his body and mind which drove him crazy with desire, satisfaction coming briefly before he was hungry for more.

Jake had had a couple of girlfriends in the past, but nothing like this. They felt like child's play to what he now experienced with Martha. She was a woman; a beautiful, sexy and captivating woman. She made him feel powerful and helpless at the same time. He couldn't get enough of her.

The night passed in a haze; Jake felt giddy, exhausted but eager for more. Martha never seemed to tire. She was confident and quickly taught him how to please her. Instinctively, she knew what he wanted and gave it to him. Suddenly, Jake cared nothing for his previous concerns about Martha and her home; he'd found Heaven here now and had no desire to be anywhere else.

He stretched as the sound of knocking travelled to his ears. Martha jumped out of bed, covering herself with a pink, silky dressing gown.

"Ignore it," he suggested, throwing back the quilt, showing her he was ready for more.

"I won't be long," she sang, disappearing into the hall.

Jake sighed and pulled himself out of bed. He might as well take the opportunity to freshen himself up a bit.

Coming out of the bathroom, Jake recognised Richard's voice. He followed the sound of the conversation into the kitchen.

Richard stood by the door, a cup cradled in his hands. Martha was standing across from him. Jake noted at once, her dressing gown was only loosely tied and as far as the expression on Richard's face was concerned, might as well not exist at all. He hurried over to her, blocking Richard's view and drawing the garment more tightly around her body. He kissed her lightly on her forehead before turning to face his friend.

"Richard, what brings you here so early in the morning?"

"Well, we were supposed to meet last night in the pub? You didn't show; the care home rang and said we can go and visit Reverend Jackson; it's not early, it's midday so I thought I'd take the initiative."

Noting that Richard's eyes had remained fixed on Martha's body the whole time he'd been speaking, Jake put his arm round her waist.

"Yeah, sorry," he began. "It completely slipped my mind. You're going now?"

Richard nodded.

"Do you mind if I take a rain-check?" Jake glanced at Martha, a smile playing on his lips.

"Oh no, mate," Richard sighed. "Apparently he'll only see me if you come along too. You can't do this to me, Jake."

Jake rolled his eyes. He felt bad for letting Richard down the previous evening but he had no desire to leave Martha now.

She made the choice for him. "You go," she suggested, "I'll be here, waiting when you get back." She turned and kissed him on the lips, her tongue slipping between his lips, ignoring Richard's presence.

When she drew away from him, Jake saw the wide grin on Richard's face. "Give me a couple of minutes," he told him. "You wait in the car, I won't be long."

Waiting until Richard had gone outside, Jake returned to the bedroom and pulled on his discarded clothes from the night before. He ran his hands through his hair.

At the back-door, he held Martha, slipping his hands beneath her dressing gown, feeling the warmth of her body beneath his fingers. "Keep the bed warm for me," he whispered into her ear.

The fresh air hit Jake like a brick; he felt dizzy but couldn't remove the grin from his lips.

Richard rolled his eyes at him as he dropped into the passenger seat. "A good night, I take it?"

Jake only continued to smile in response as the car moved off.

His doze lasted the duration of the journey and Jake felt even more sleepy as Richard nudged him awake.

"Pull yourself together," he ordered.

Like a zombie, Jake followed Richard into reception and then upstairs to room seven. Seeing Reverend Jackson's beaming smile, Jake felt the least he could do was shake himself up a bit and appear more interested than he'd managed so far.

"Sorry about yesterday," the old man began. "If I get too much excitement, these old lungs start wheezing," he explained, tapping his chest.

"Don't worry, it's no problem," Richard said. "So, what were you saying yesterday about the old castle, on Bailey Hill?" he prompted.

Reverend Jackson became thoughtful; Jake was worried he would phase out on them again and they'd be here all day. An image of Martha crept into his head which he fought hard against to eliminate it.

"The castle was ancient but drew people to the area. It was a time when folks knew no better and believed in goblins and ghosts, witches too," the old man continued, his eyes fixed as though he could picture the scene before him.

"Any woman of a certain type, or appearance, was at risk if someone became suspicious of her. It didn't take much: curing a cold, owning a cat or simply picking particular herbs could result in her being accused of witchcraft."

Jake stifled a yawn and glanced at Richard. He gave Jake a frown and turned his attention back to Reverend Jackson.

"You must realise, it's impossible to verify any of this, records weren't kept in those days so it's only word of mouth, through the centuries, which keeps these tales alive." He looked at Richard who gave an encouraging nod.

"A woman was accused of meddling with evil spirits. A crop failed or a child was suddenly taken ill, some such event occurred and it was easiest to place the blame on her. Trouble is, everyone was frightened of her then, you see, no one wanted anything to do with her, didn't want her near them, especially with night falling and everything becoming darker and more threatening."

"They cried for her blood but didn't want her within the walls of the castle. Just outside the gates stood a birch tree. It had been dead for years and nobody took any notice of it but suddenly, the old tree became a suitable place for a witch to spend the night before she went on trial for her crimes."

The old man paused, slightly breathless and pointed to the jug of water. Richard jumped up and poured a glass, passing it to the priest.

He drank thirstily, his hand clutching the empty beaker, dropped onto the bed by his side. For a moment, he appeared to be sleeping. Then, his eyes opened, seeming to sparkle with excitement.

"There she was: strapped to the tree and abandoned by the people who had once been her neighbours and friends. The wind began to whip up as a storm approached. A gale tore round the castle walls; rain battered the ground and lightning lit up the night sky. And through all of this, that poor woman was helpless: exposed to the elements, her arms bleeding from the ropes, her back hard against the bark of the dead tree, and alone."

He shook his head. Jake glanced at Richard again, he appeared to be doodling down the margin of the open book on his lap. When he saw Jake looking at him, he rolled his eyes and focused his attention back on the priest.

"I can't imagine what went through that poor woman's head that night. Who knows whether she even believed in witchcraft, yet alone cavorted with the devil himself? It didn't matter, just to be accused meant certain death." He shook his head slowly.

"It was during that night, the storm was violent and a flash of lightning struck the tree to which the woman was tied; it began to smoulder. As smoke rose into the air, a curse spewed from the woman's mouth. Whilst the incomprehensible words poured forth, disappearing into the chaos raging around her, the most terrible thing began to take place."

Jake was spell-bound. Reverend Jackson looked from one man to the other as if to check he had their full attention. Richard scratched his chin, refraining from catching Jake's gaze.

"So, what happened?" Richard drawled.

"As the woman continued to chant her curse on the castle and its inhabitants, her body drenched and icy, smoke filling her weary lungs, the tree began to devour her."

Richard snorted. "What? You're telling me the tree ate her?"

"Think of it like that, if you must," the old man told him. "I prefer to consider the tree absorbed her energy, both positive and negative. Birch trees have long been associated with death; rather than her becoming an empty shell, she was moulded into its body. By the time the storm had abated the following morning and people began to go about their business, the woman was dead. However, where her body had so recently been displayed as a deterrent to others, only her arms and legs remained, as if the tree had gained limbs. As for the tree, for the first time in years, new buds sprung from long-dead branches."

"Of course, it created widespread fear as news of the woman's demise, and the tree's re-generation grew. It was difficult to dispel superstition and terror when the evidence was so clear. Even when the tree was chopped down, leaves continued to grow."

"Why didn't they just burn it?" Jake asked.

"Oh, they tried. Although it was a tree, it wouldn't burn, almost like an invisible cloak protected it from further destruction. Besides, even if the tree was destroyed, it's possible the evil spirit which lurked inside it, had long enough to extend its roots deep into the hillside. They could hardly obliterate the whole woodland, which would have been much larger back then."

"And is the tree still there?" Jake asked.

Reverend Jackson held out his hands. "Who knows?"

Jake looked at Richard: "What do you think?"

Richard shrugged. "Why does it matter what I think? A witch died, a tree was cut down. The castle disappeared centuries ago. It's a story, there are hundreds of those. Why should it have anything to do with this girl's death, and Amy's, of course?"

"It could be a link," Jake mumbled.

"If you'll let me finish," the old priest muttered.

They both turned their attention back to him and fell silent.

"You're right, the castle no longer exists, hasn't been there for a very long time but consider this … Before the last of the inhabitants left, another story unfolded."

Richard whistled, rolling his eyes to the ceiling and folded his notepad shut.

"Sorry," Jake apologised for his friend's rudeness, "please, continue." He scowled at Richard and turned back to the old man.

"The story goes … a girl disappeared from the castle, she was the daughter of a soldier so a hunt for her ensued. Yet, no matter where they looked or how hard they searched, nothing was found of her. Then, several years later, another girl disappeared from the nearby village."

"And I suppose she wasn't found either?" Richard enquired.

"You're right," Reverend Jackson told him, "however, another girl wandered into the village."

"So, what?" Richard asked.

"If you would kindly stop interrupting me, and let me finish?"

"Sorry," Richard conceded, "please carry on." He pulled a face at Jake, which Jake chose to ignore.

"Someone in the village recognised the girl, but it wasn't the girl who had recently vanished; it was the girl who had disappeared from the castle, all those years before." He looked from one to the other of his listeners triumphantly.

After a moment's silence, Richard cleared his throat. "I'm sorry, but am I missing something here?"

Reverend Jackson smiled. "Although many years had passed since the girl had disappeared, when she walked into the village, she looked exactly the same as she had when she went missing. She should have been a grown woman but she was still a seven-year-old girl when she returned."

Jake stared at the old man. It sounded incredible and he wasn't quite sure how they could link the tale to what had occurred more recently. Yet, it definitely made it more than just a coincidence as far as he was concerned.

"So, what happened to the girl who had originally gone from the village? Did she turn up too?" Richard asked.

"Well," he began again, "once more, nothing was heard of her for years, then, one day, she walked into a nearby village."

"And I suppose, she was still just a child?" Richard hazarded.

Reverend Jackson nodded. "You've got it. The legend went, that the tree took a victim whenever it needed to regenerate more energy, then, in order for that body to regain their human life and form, a new corpse was required to take their place. It's almost as if the tree took one life in order to give birth to another."

"So, there is always a missing child?" Jake asked.

"That's right," the priest confirmed. "But it is always a female victim." He shrugged, "perhaps it is the female's ability to give birth to young which is needed by the tree?"

Richard glanced at his watch and cleared his throat, as he stood up.

"It's been really interesting," he told the slightly bewildered priest. "I do, however, have another meeting I am expected at. It's been lovely meeting you." He held his hand out.

Jake stood up too and after they had both bid the old man 'goodbye', they returned to the car.

"You were really rude to him," Jake told Richard as they drove down the driveway.

"Oh, come on, Jake. You don't seriously believe anything he told us? The guy's a half-wit!"

"Whatever you think of what he said, it doesn't excuse being rude to him. After all, you're the one who wanted to speak to the man."

Richard glanced at Jake. He lifted one hand off the steering wheel, holding it up defensively. "Okay, I'm sorry, I shouldn't have been rude to him. He probably didn't notice though."

Jake shook his head slowly. He was pretty sure Reverend Jackson was a lot more aware of what went on around him than Richard was giving him credit for.

"What are you going to do now?" Jake asked, as they slipped into the flow of traffic.

Richard cast a brief look at Jake. "Me? Nothing? Sweet F.A.! Been a complete waste of my time as far as I'm concerned. I'm just sorry I wasted your time too, Jake."

"You don't believe him, I take it?"

Richard snorted, then looked at Jake briefly once more. "You're not telling me you do?"

Jake shrugged. "Who knows? I'm sure there's plenty of fiction in there; but you never know, some of it might be true?" he suggested tentatively.

"Oh, come on!" Richard exclaimed. "You're telling me this girl is going to turn up again in a few years from now as right as rain? Even though the police have her body? Even though this is the twenty first century? Even though everyone knows witches don't exist, they never did? How far do you think my young career as a journalist will last if I go to the local paper telling them this is what I want to print?" He smacked his hands on the steering wheel, grinning and shaking his head.

Jake turned his attention to the outside of the car. Clearly, he and Richard were on different wave lengths. Of course, he didn't believe everything Reverend Jackson had told them, yet it was niggling at him and he didn't want to dismiss it as quickly as Richard had obviously done. He needed some time to think, alone.

"Can you drop me off here?" Jake suddenly asked.

"Oh, you're not angry at me, are you?" Richard demanded.

"No, I just need some fresh air," Jake lied, although after the stuffiness of the care home and his lack of sleep from the night before, it couldn't do any harm.

Richard glanced in the rear-view mirror before he indicated and pulled into the kerb. "You sure you'll be okay from here?"

Jake glanced around. "Yeah, this is on the bus route," he replied. "I'll walk for a bit and then catch a bus back home."

Richard grinned and gave him a wave before easing his car back into the flow of traffic.

Jake stepped back, out of the way of other pedestrians, and sighed. He had no idea what he believed, or what to think. It was totally crazy, Richard was right, but Jake didn't want to be too hasty in dismissing it.

He began walking. Eventually he came across a coffee bar. A dose of caffeine was suddenly very appealing.

Taking a seat by the window, Jake pulled his mobile out of his pocket and sent a brief text to his mum to keep her happy. He lay his phone on the table and took a sip from his cup.

Momentarily, Jake closed his eyes. His head was swimming with a combination of tiredness and hunger, as well as the caffeine he had just ingested. A waitress brought his panini to the table and Jake bit into it quickly, enjoying the burst of flavours which exploded in his mouth.

He knew the old priest's story was fantastical. However, there had to be something which could link the legend to what had happened to Amy. Perhaps he would go to the library himself the following day and scour old, local books, records and newspapers. Richard may not be interested but Jake considered it would be ironic if it was the non-journalist who discovered a scoop.

There was still a blur surrounding it all. Jake cursed that he had been so young when Amy died. He'd not paid much attention to his mum's theories, and even though Amy had been his sister, Jake hadn't bothered reading the newspapers or listened to any gossip.

Feeling a little more human, Jake strolled to the next bus stop and waited for a ride back to the village. His thoughts swung between a desperation to get back to Martha, although he wasn't sure where he would summon the energy from to compete with her apparent endless supply. He also wanted to speak to people, to listen to conversations and learn whether there was any other such talk as they'd heard from Reverend Jackson earlier.

Watching for his bus stop as the bus dragged itself up the hill, Jake caught a glance of a pedestrian standing against a dry-stone wall, waiting for the bus to pass. As the bus passed them, Jake saw it was the girl he'd seen in the woods after the freak storm.

In an instant, he jumped up and was calling for the driver to stop the vehicle. He rushed along the aisle, careering from side to side as the bus rolled to a halt. Shouting his gratitude, Jake jumped onto the verge as the doors closed again behind him.

Immediately, Jake was aware of her fear. Panic painted her face as she turned to hurry back in the direction she'd just come from.

"No, please, wait," Jake called after her. "I don't want to hurt you, I just need to speak to you."

Jake stopped moving towards her and held out his hands. "Please," he begged. "I won't come any closer. Just listen and then, I swear, I'll turn around and walk away from you."

Taking her hesitation as mild acceptance, Jake racked his brain as to how to begin without confirming her suspicions he must be a weirdo.

"I don't suppose your name is Amy, by any chance?" He asked.

She shook her head, frowning. "Amelia," she told him.

"I must apologise for scaring you before; I don't blame you for telling the police about me, I'd have probably mentioned it too," Jake said.

Amelia gave a small smile.

"I lived in the village when I was a child, we moved away when I was ten and it's the first time I've been back. The day you saw me, I decided to explore the woods, I assumed I'd remember the way, but I lost my bearings and when you came across me I was starting to panic a bit, I'm afraid," Jake explained.

She nodded and took a small step backwards.

"I really mean you no harm," Jake said quickly. "I wanted to ask you a simple question: do you recognise me? Not from the other day, but had you ever seen me before?"

He was finding it odd talking to this stranger who looked identical to his long-dead sister. Struggling against his urge to reach out and hug her, Jake hoped he looked harmless.

Watching her face as she made a valiant effort to take in his appearance, Jake searched for any sign of recognition in her expression. She opened her mouth to speak, then closed it again and shook her head.

"Look, I know it sounds crazy, but you are exactly like my sister. Her name was Amy. She was only fifteen when she was found dead, in the woods over there. I'm sure you can understand why your appearance there gave me such a scare."

For a moment, Amelia almost looked sympathetic. Then a veil of indifference swept across her face. "Can I go now?"

Jake closed his eyes for a moment and sighed. When he looked again, Amelia was already walking away from him. "Thank you," he called after her retreating figure.

She didn't acknowledge him. Jake leant against the wall, hands in his pockets, staring at the ground in front of his feet.

Of course it had been a foolish idea. He'd been so ready to believe the old priest and slot Amy's death into the story, Jake realised he'd suspended every ounce of sanity he possessed. But why? He'd always been happy to accept the police account of what had happened, despite his mum's ideas to the contrary. He wondered how she'd react if he told her about Reverend Jackson and what he'd told them. Weighing up both sides, he concluded it would do no good if he shared it with her, in fact, it would simply rake up old memories and dormant pain.

Turning round and looking over the wall and across the field beyond it, Jake stared at the wooded hillside. What is your secret? Then he laughed. Do you even have a secret? Or am I becoming as crazy as my mother and that old man?

The late afternoon sun was shining above the hilltop; beams streaked across the sky as the orb lay partially hidden from his view. Beneath it, leaves left clinging to branches sparkled like gold in the path of the sunlight. The scene brought Amy into Jake's mind: she would have identified the trees for him, led him along the footpaths and pointed out familiar plants and birds to him. She'd have known where to find burrows and setts and have mocked him for daring to suggest a cityscape was preferable. What would she have made of the old man's tale? What would she want him to do?

Jake's heart felt heavy. He wished he'd known her better, that they'd had more time to share. It pained Jake to realise he couldn't answer either of the questions which had come into his mind because he had no idea what his sister would have thought or done.

He focused his attention back on the hillside. As the leaves rustled in the breeze under the watchful eye of the sun, they rippled like a river, heading down towards the village. Jake glanced across at the churchyard where Amy's body laid at rest; then his eyes followed an invisible path to where he knew Bailey Hill lay just to the west of the church.

If the birch tree, Reverend Jackson had referred to, had been felled where it stood, if it did still exist, it couldn't be far from where the castle had once been. It wasn't far off his route he'd have to take to get to Martha's.

Jake stepped back from the wall and began walking up towards High Bradfield; he smiled to himself as he imagined what Richard would say if he knew what he was about to do.

The gate into the churchyard creaked as it swung slowly open. A couple of sheep in the graveyard stopped chewing to observe his presence, before they obviously classed him as no threat and resumed their meal.

Jake strolled past the church, following the path between the graves to the area beyond where the more recent gravestones stood.

In the far corner lay the small wooden gate which led into the woods; it was swathed in plastic ribbon, left by the police. Unsure whether the woods had been re-opened to the public, Jake stepped across a broken section of the church perimeter wall instead, where stones lay strewn across the ground.

Unsure whether the temperature really did drop when he moved into the woods, or whether it was a result of his over-active imagination which made him shudder, Jake hesitated.

Silence. No sound whatsoever. He could hear only the thumping of his heart inside his chest. Jake ran his hand through his hair and looked slowly around him.

There were two mounds, he wasn't sure whether the castle had occupied both or whether a much wider area had been built upon, no evidence remained of any former habitation.

Strolling around the perimeter of both steep, but small hills, Jake kept a look out for any fallen trees. He had no idea how long a dead tree would remain intact but there seemed to be nothing here which could possibly be the tree the priest had referred to. Yes, there were broken branches, a pile of cut logs and deep undergrowth around the edge of the woodland, but nothing stood out to him. Jake wasn't sure what he'd been expecting and he couldn't help the dull thud of disappointment he felt.

Needing to cross the bridge in the woods to get to the footpath which led back up to Martha's, Jake turned his back on Bailey Hill and headed deeper into the trees. His head was filled with thoughts of the priest's tale. It was strange to imagine all those events occurring on the ground upon which he now stood, centuries before. Pausing to look around him, Jake tried to picture the scene as it would have appeared back then.

A sudden thought came to him: of course, it would have looked very different then; there wouldn't have been woods surrounding the castle. For protection purposes, they'd have wanted a clear view to spot any approaching enemies with plenty of notice to prepare for an attack. A single tree wouldn't have been a problem, but a whole forest would have hidden approaching foe. What if the fallen tree had been moved? Maybe they'd dragged it further downhill, out of the way and to rid themselves of the birch which had seemed to consume the evil of the witch.

Jake found himself smiling, feeling more hopeful that the trunk could still be here somewhere. Then he stopped; now the entire hillside was covered in woodland. It could take him weeks to scour the entire site. And how would he find a birch tree without leaves to help him identify it?

Crossing the bridge, Jake glanced in both directions. Perhaps he could spare a little time now, he considered, as he found his feet leading him downhill and away from Martha's.

He really must be losing his mind, Jake pondered in the fading light. Paths crossed and disappeared into the undergrowth, he had to convince himself that the eerie silence was natural for the setting, that he'd spent too much time surrounding himself with people and noise to find the quiet, natural.

As he stumbled over a tree root he'd failed to notice on the path, Jake put his hands out to stop himself falling and slammed them against a tree. Winded for a moment, he closed his eyes, stretching his shoulders back. Into his head flew an image of Amy, she was crying, covered in mud mixed with blood. Unable to walk, he saw her dragging her body along the path where he stood now. But it wasn't her voice he could hear; it was Martha's. A mix of coaxing and teasing spewed from her lips. His mum's accusations about Martha's involvement in his sister's death came into his head. Immediately, Jake dismissed it, his body shivered.

The part of his brain which wanted him to be in bed with Martha must have projected her voice into his thoughts of his sister, Jake decided, trying hopelessly to separate the two aspects of his imagination. The intrigued part of him simply couldn't think of the priest's tale without it somehow involving his sister's death.

Suddenly aware of his senses once more, Jake realised he could hear a vigorous shuffling sound. He was unable to see anything but he began to follow the direction the noise was coming from.

It gradually got louder and more hurried at his approach. Jake ducked down as he fought against thoughts of murderers and ghosts creeping into his head.

Laughing to himself, holding out his hand and gently whispering, Jake advanced towards the rabbit which had come into his view. Its rear legs were caught up in some police tape which was wound onto a fallen tree trunk. As the rabbit had struggled, the tape had tightened. Clearly, Jake's approach had sent the rabbit into a renewed frenzy of struggling and it looked at him with enormous eyes.

Jake took hold of the tape and carefully snapped it from the trunk. Holding it firmly, he then began to unwind it from the rabbit's legs, pausing each time the rabbit kicked out furiously. The task was tiresome but absorbed Jake's mind as he tried to work quickly for the sake of the exhausted animal.

With a final tug of the tape, the rabbit was freed and disappeared in a flash beneath the trunk. Jake sat back on his haunches, winding the tape into a small ball. He'd not heard the rabbit escape from beyond the trunk so assumed there must be a warren below the safety of this wooden canopy. He peered into the darkness below the tree; despite the lack of visibility, Jake got the impression there was a deep space beneath it.

Something glistened, catching his eye. Reaching into the gap, Jake felt the damp earth with his fingertips. The soil was cold and loose, falling quickly between his fingers. Tiny feet scurried across the back of his hand, making him shiver.

His hand swept across the littered ground blindly. Dead leaves crumbled beneath his touch, small twigs rolled and snapped; Jake imagined them as skinny fingers lying in wait…

A clammy web brushed against his touch like a skin clinging to his own. As Jake's fingers wrapped around a hard, tiny object, his hand curled into a fist. Before he could withdraw his forearm from the hole, he felt a strong pull from beneath his grasp. When Jake tried to draw up his hand, something pulled it back downwards. Whatever held him, kept his fist clenched tightly, he could feel the blood draining from his hand as his fingernails dug into his palm.

Jake rested his free hand against the tree trunk and used all his strength to push against the tree, trying to free himself. He felt like the rabbit: the harder he pulled back, the firmer the invisible grip pulled him against the trunk.

Twisting his arm, backwards and forwards, Jake heard the sound of his own voice as he cried out in anger and frustration. The pull came from, what seemed like, a large, firm hand trying to drag him down under the trunk; his hand was that of a child by comparison.

Fingers began to extend along his arm, nails clawed at his skin. Jake dug his trainers more firmly into the soil, trying to lever himself back from the side of the dead tree.

A terrible stench filled his nostrils like putrid meat. Whispered voices floated on the air around his head, although Jake knew he was alone.

Suddenly, he yelled a cry of: "Help!" The hold on his arm disappeared in an instant and Jake fell with a sharp thud, back against the ground.

Breathlessly, he examined his arm and hand. Wiping away the smeared mud, Jake saw it was mixed with the red of his blood. Three angry welts had broken the skin along his forearm; they were raw and already he could feel them throbbing in pain.

He turned the small object lying in his palm. As he cleared it of dirt, Jake realised it was a ring, chunky but small, it was a signet ring with the letter A against an outline of a skull. It was the kind of ornament he could imagine a Hell's Angel sporting, along with an array of others of a similar style. It was ugly and he let it drop back onto the ground dismissively.

Wiping his other arm across his face, slowly Jake stood up. His legs shook slightly; he rested the weight of his body against the trunk for support.

Jake looked around the, now, peaceful woodland. He'd not realised the darkness before now. He needed to get back to Martha's. Setting one foot in front of the other, Jake headed uphill, wondering what he looked like. What on earth had happened? Had he inadvertently discovered the tree he'd been searching for?

The pain and soreness in his arm was increasing; his arm felt like it was on fire now, despite the chilliness of the evening air. Jake wiped his forehead; it was damp with sweat.

It was with a huge sense of relief he stepped over the stile, leaving the woods behind him. From the footpath, Jake could now see the faint glow of light from Martha's bungalow, guiding him homewards.

Practically collapsing through the back door, Jake pulled himself upright as Martha turned and stared at him.

"What on earth …?"

She moved quickly to his side, gently putting her hands beneath his injured arm and examining the wounds. "Did you get attacked by an animal?"

Jake shook his head, pointing at the taps above the sink.

Martha ran him a glass of cold water. Jake took it and drank quickly.

"It's nothing," he muttered, surprised at how bad the cuts looked now under the artificial light of the kitchen. The blood contrasted with the paleness of the surrounding skin, which Jake had considered nicely tanned. He realised his clothes were littered with leaf debris and soil too.

"Doesn't look like nothing," Martha scolded. "Let me see what I've got I can use to clean that up."

Jake said nothing as she disappeared. He leant his body against the work surface and closed his eyes for a moment. At once, his head began spinning; Jake opened his eyes again as Martha came back. She ran some warm water into the sink and tore off pieces of cotton wool from a larger piece in a clear, plastic bag.

"This is going to hurt," she advised as she held his arm over the sink, squeezing out some water from a piece of the cotton wool.

As the water dripped onto his arm, Jake jerked back. Martha held his arm firmly. As she slowly began to bathe the wounds, Jake closed his eyes.

"Are you going to tell me what happened?" Martha asked after a while.

Jake considered how to reply. The truth would sound incredible and he knew he was unable to tell her what had attacked him; after all, he had no idea himself.

He realised Martha was now still and looking directly at him. Jake shrugged. The pounding of the pain in his arm was making him feel sick.

"Have you got something I can take for this?" he asked, pointing at the lacerations. "It's agony."

Martha glanced at his face. "I'll find you something," she told him and began searching through a drawer.

The tablets looked as if they'd been in their box for years; Jake didn't care, anything which might relieve some of the pain he was experiencing would be welcome. He downed the pills with the last of the water. Martha had finished dealing with his injuries and was washing round the sink with clean water. Jake stared at the angry marks on his arm. Whatever had attacked him was deadly. Any longer, stuck against that tree, and he'd have been lucky to escape with his arm still intact, he realised.

What on earth could it be down there? Surely no wild animal could behave in such a way, or create such tears in his skin. He peered down more closely at his arm. The wounds looked deep. If his mum was here, Jake was sure she'd have him on his way to A&E by now. He wondered whether he was up to date with his tetanus jabs.

Looking at it was beginning to make him feel nauseous. Seeing as Martha was still busying herself at the sink, Jake went through to the sitting room and collapsed onto the sofa. He kicked off his shoes and laid his head down on a cushion. Closing his eyes to try and stop the room from spinning around him, Jake accepted the abyss of sleep gladly.

Chapter 7

Grey light penetrated through the drawn curtains as the moisture on the cushion beneath his cheek brought Jake gradually back to his senses. Groaning quietly, he wiped his mouth and edged himself onto his back.

He felt stiff, his arm was like a dead weight and glowing with heat. Realising he'd slept through the night, Jake swallowed uncomfortably, his tongue furry and his teeth rough. He needed water but he was loath to move yet. Recalling how dizzy he'd felt as he'd fallen asleep, Jake rubbed his temples and let his hand wipe across his face. He could do with a shower, fresh clothes too and his last proper meal was a distant memory.

Holding his arm up in front of his face, Jake studied the rough landscape of his forearm. There was a slight sheen now, where the bleeding had ceased; small pools of clear liquid wept from the tender skin. It was fascinating, yet abhorrent, drawing his eyes and thoughts back to what had happened in the woods the previous night.

A slight sound made Jake look up. Martha was watching him from the armchair. Her face was composed, her hands resting in her lap. She looked as though she had been waiting for him to wake up; could she have been there all night?

Slowly, Jake pulled himself up until he was sitting. "Sorry, I clearly needed that sleep."

"It's fine," she replied. "How's your arm?"

"Looks better already," Jake replied. "I probably stink, I'll grab a shower if that's okay with you?"

Martha nodded, smiling.

Jake let the water soak away his weariness. Holding his arm gently against the tiled wall to avoid the unnecessary sting from the flow of water, he stood with his eyes closed, appreciating the gradual rejuvenation of his body.

Once he was dressed, Jake got himself a drink and a sandwich and stood in the kitchen staring out of the window as he ate. The sky wasn't much brighter than when he'd woken up. A light drizzle fell, tiny streams of rain ran down the outside of the glass. His eyes looked from the surface of the window, to the bare yard beyond.

Inevitably, Jake's mind returned to the woods. Lost in thought, Martha's arms, wrapping themselves around his waist, made him jump and he dropped the last piece of his sandwich onto the work surface.

"Sorry," she sighed as he turned to face her.

Her smiling face eased him at once. Jake held her in his arms and rested his head on hers, inhaling the floral scent of her hair.

"I guess I'm not the easiest of guests," Jake said at length.

Martha pulled back slightly and looked at his face, smiling. "You still haven't told me what happened last night," she reminded him.

Jake tried to draw her back to him but she pulled further back until she'd shaken herself completely free of his embrace.

"Okay," he conceded, "but can we have a hot drink first?"

"I'll make it," Martha suggested. "You go and sit down; I'll bring it through."

Jake sunk into the armchair and closed his eyes. Whilst he did feel somewhat refreshed, he wished his arm would stop the burning sensation for a bit. He longed just to sleep again, but knew he owed Martha some sort of explanation, and didn't imagine for one minute she was going to forget about it.

He'd almost dozed off by the time she put the tray down on the coffee table. His eyes opened at the sound and for a moment Jake had to think about where he was.

Gratefully, he accepted his tea and took a sip before putting it down on the table, noting the shakiness of his grip.

Martha sat on the sofa looking at him expectantly. Jake gave a weak smile and began telling her about Richard and their visit to Reverend Jackson.

Her face was impossible to read. Jake stumbled over his story, hesitating, unsure whether she was still listening or had switched off from his narrative. He speeded up, worried she was bored but Martha's steely gaze remained static.

"So, what happened to your arm?" she asked, when he'd finished telling her about the old priest.

Jake hesitated. "I went through the woods; I thought I could find the tree from the story."

"And did you?"

"I'm not sure," Jake muttered, shaking his head. "There's an old, fallen trunk. I can't tell what type of tree it is but there's something strange about it."

"Strange?" Martha prompted.

Jake rolled his eyes and ran his hand through his hair, leaning forward in his chair. "I'm sure I'd been there before; I seem to find my way to the same place every time I go into those woods. I thought I'd got myself lost but then I spotted a shiny object, on the ground. When I reached down to get it, something grabbed my hand."

"The tree?" Martha grinned.

"Look, I know it sounds ridiculous, but hear me out."

She held up her hands in surrender.

"I couldn't get free and it was pulling me closer, down under the trunk. Then it began clawing at my arm; I thought it was going to rip me to shreds." Jake paused, breathless.

"You're saying, something grabbed you from under the tree and tried to drag you down?" Martha gazed at him.

Jake adjusted his position. "Yeah."

She laughed. Jake waited. Eventually she stopped when she realised he was looking at her.

"That's impossible," Martha stated.

Whatever Jake had expected her to say, he hadn't been ready for such a level tone of response. "Why? What d'you mean?"

Martha frowned, hesitating. "Nothing," she replied.

"No, come on," Jake prompted. "You said that as though what happened was all perfectly normal. You can't leave it at that."

Martha looked annoyed. "It's nothing, Jake," she snapped, jumping up from the sofa.

Jake followed her into the kitchen. "I've just let myself sound like an idiot by telling you my story," he began. "Whatever you say can't be any worse. Have you ever seen something in the woods?"

She turned around to face him. "Let it go, Jake," Martha whispered, almost inaudibly.

"What's wrong?" Jake asked, taking hold of her hand.

"Stop!" she screeched, shaking her hand free of his. "You're just like your mother."

"My mum? What's she got to do with anything?" Jake had been ready for her laughter at him, even her questions and disbelief. But this was something else; he couldn't understand why she was the one acting defensively.

"You're both obsessed with those woods. She used to rant and rave about all sorts of crazy stories and wouldn't let them go. Now, you're doing the same thing. Have you listened to yourself?" She shook her head, wiping away tears of frustration from her eyes.

Frowning, Jake studied her face. "You asked me to tell you what happened to me last night. Even though I knew how crazy it sounded, I trust you enough to share what happened as best I could. You can tell me it's mad or unbelievable, but don't get angry at me and drag my mum into this conversation."

Martha stared at him. Jake tried to maintain his gaze at her, but he turned away, leaning heavily on his good arm for support from the kitchen unit.

"She sent you, didn't she?" Martha asked quietly. "All this," she cried, holding out her arms, "has been a game to you. 'Enough time has passed, let's make Martha pay for what she did'," she taunted.

Slowly, Jake turned back to face her and took a couple of steps forward until he was standing close enough to feel her breath on his face. "What Martha? What did you do?"

The blood seemed to turn to ice inside his body, an involuntary shiver swept through him but Jake kept his eyes fixed on Martha's unflinching gaze.

For a moment, he thought she was going to smile but her eyes darkened again. "Don't play with me, Jake. You don't know how foolish that could prove to be."

Jake cocked his head slightly and took a step back. "I think we're having two conversations here," he said at length. "You wanted to know what happened to my arm and I've told you. I can't explain what occurred, and I know how fantastical it sounds; you aren't obliged to believe me. But, where has all this anger come from? I wasn't aware I had accused you of anything, or that I was playing with you. Do you think I got you into bed just for some kind of dare?" He could feel the irritation pushing up through his chest. Suddenly Martha was looking like the small girl who had stood in the playground, defiantly challenging anyone to take on the new girl. She'd had them all in awe of her back then, being wilful and bold. They'd never met anyone quite like her before.

"I don't know what to think, Jake," she said. "I don't know whether I can trust you." Her voice was calm. Jake wasn't sure if she sounded sad or resigned. He gazed at her full, red lips, slightly parted. Her long, dark lashes were damp and her eyes were innocent again.

Unable to help himself, Jake stepped forward and kissed her lips, pushing his body against hers, his hands holding her head. For a moment, he thought he felt her relax and return his kiss. Then, a sudden, sharp pain threw him backwards, his hands drawn at once to his bleeding lip.

Jake stared at her. "You bitch!"

Her eyes danced. He looked down at the bright red blood on his fingertips. Probing his lip with his tongue, Jake could feel the swelling on his lower lip already.

"What the hell was that for? You could've just said 'no'."

"Don't play with me, Jake," Martha warned. "You don't know what you're getting into with this detective stuff. Go back to your perfect, little world and leave things which don't concern you alone. You can never understand what's in those woods and you'd be a fool to even try."

They stared at each other. Martha's face was a blank; she seemed able to turn her emotions on and off like the flick of a switch. Jake's mind was racing so fast, he thought his head was in danger of imploding.

"You don't seem surprised then, by what I experienced? I thought you'd laugh at me, or accuse me of lying. I'm sorry if I've offended you, in some way, but I want to find out what's out there, Martha. If Amy's death wasn't an accident, I think I have a right to know."

"Is that why you came back in the first place? To discover what happened to your sister? After all this time?"

Jake nodded. "Ever since we left here, I've had dreams about Amy. I know I was only a kid when she died and I wasn't there, but in my dreams, I saw her, sometimes you were there too," he paused, looking at Martha apologetically. "I thought if I came back, it might stop the dreams. I just want to put it behind me."

"So, just like your mum, you came looking for me? Thinking you could blame Amy's death on someone else?" Her eyes were like small, poisoned darts, shooting Jake with arrows of hatred.

"No," Jake cried, emphatically. "I never paid any attention to what my mum said about Amy's death. I know she was mourning and clutching at any idea about her death to ease her sense of guilt for Amy being out there alone, in the first place."

"I don't know why my mum never liked you," Jake continued quickly. "But I'd hardly have kept in touch with you if I believed for one minute you had anything to do with my sister's death, would I?"

Martha looked at him, hesitating. "I don't know if I can trust you, Jake."

He risked a step towards her. "I love you, Martha. I'm not the kind of guy who jumps into bed with a girl at any opportunity. You mean so much to me, I wouldn't want to risk losing you."

They looked at each other. "Say something?" Jake prompted her.

For a brief moment, her eyes looked at him beseechingly. Then, Martha pushed her clenched fists to her face, hiding herself from his gaze.

"Martha?" Jake asked, gently reaching out and touching her shoulder.

She wriggled free of his reach, waving her arms and knocking his hand away. "You say those words too easily. You're here because your mum sent you and thought you'd jump into my bed at the same time. Well, I'm telling you, Jake, you mean nothing to me. You're a joke, you always were and you haven't changed one bit."

Her words flew at him: small stones thrown with great force. Jake felt his face redden, incomprehension mixed with frustration that he seemed unable to break through her invisible barrier. He'd thought they shared a silent understanding between themselves, years of continued contact, surely, had to count for something. He wasn't about to give up and walk away when he'd come this far.

"Look," he began. "I can see this isn't easy for you, so I'll find somewhere else to stay, if you like. But you have to know, I'm going to hang around until I find out whether there is anything in those woods that was responsible for Amy's death."

Jake was startled to hear his own words spoken. Until they were out of his mouth, he'd not realised just how embroiled in this mystery he was. Maybe he was starting to sound like his mum but he'd not be able to live with himself if he simply turned and walked away. With or without Martha's support, Jake wasn't about to give up.

She looked at him defiantly. Any surprise she might have felt, was well-hidden. Fully aware of Martha's individuality, this was the first occasion Jake felt such frustration at her indifference and coldness. Maybe this was the only time he had experienced being the victim of her obstinacy.

"You do whatever you like, Jake," Martha replied. "It doesn't bother me. You're a fool though." She turned her back on him and began clearing away things left on the work surface.

"What is it with you?" Jake demanded, reaching out to touch her elbow. "What do you know?"

Martha glared at him, shaking his hand away. "You've seen its strength," she stated, pointing towards his arm. "You really think you can change anything after all these years?"

"You sound as if you already knew about the old priest's story, as if you believe it." Jake hated having her chilly attitude directed at himself. He'd always known it was there, seen numerous examples of it being directed at others. If Martha did know anything, and he was sure she did, he'd rather have her support than her disapproval, after all, it was Martha who had brought him back here.

"You're playing with fire, Jake. You can't win and you have no idea whether you'll make things far worse."

A sudden knocking at the door made both their heads spin towards the direction of the sound. Through the frosted glass, Jake recognised the outline of his mum. After a glance at Martha, he reached forward and pulled the door open.

"Mum!" He exclaimed, trying to calm his voice. "What are you doing here?" He asked, peering past her to see if Pasquale was with her.

"Nice to see you too! I told you, Jake, if you didn't keep in contact, and weren't home in three days, I'd be back." Marion stood looking at her son, fully aware of Martha's close proximity.

"But it hasn't been three days, has it?" Jake whined.

Suddenly, Marion spotted Jake's injured arm: "What on earth is that?" She demanded. "Did she do this?" She hissed, looking past his shoulder. Pushing her son back, Marion stepped into the kitchen, glaring at Martha as soon as she had her in full view.

Marion turned back to face Jake. Carefully, she lifted his arm and studied the wounds. "These are really nasty," she told him. "You need stitches." Looking up at his face, she became aware of the cold atmosphere between these two youngsters and realised her timing had probably not been great.

"What's going on here?" She asked Jake.

"We were just in the middle of something," he replied quietly, glancing across at Martha, surprised by her silence at his mother's intrusion.

"Well, I'm sorry if I interrupted anything," she replied briefly. "But I'm here until you tell me what happened to your arm. Are you ready to come home now?" She looked at him, expectantly.

Jake shook his head slowly. "I have things to deal with here," he told her. "I'm not a child any more, I can come and go as I please."

Marion snorted. "Clearly, you're not great at looking after yourself."

"Stop fussing, Mum. I'm an adult. I have unfinished business and I'm not coming back home until it's sorted."

"Go with her, Jake," Martha said wearily, speaking at last. "There's nothing for you to do here and you'll be safer leaving this place."

Jake and Marion stared at her. Marion glanced at her son. "Tell me what's going on," she said cautiously. "What does she mean: 'you'll be safer'?"

He looked from his mum to Martha and back again. "It's complicated, and I'm not entirely sure myself."

"Well, you must know how you got that," she replied, pointing at his arm.

"Not really," Jake muttered.

"Martha, please," he begged, turning his attention back towards her. "I don't want us to fight. I need your help."

Jake ignored the snort of disgust from his mum. He tried taking Martha's hand and this time she didn't push him away.

Marion stepped forward, standing next to her son, refusing to be excluded from whatever was happening here. She'd not stood by her daughter, and she wasn't about to let her son down too.

"We don't need her, Jake," she said. "You've got me now; we don't need her," she repeated.

Jake turned on her. "You don't have any idea what you're talking about. You can't come in here and take over. This is Martha's home, she's my girlfriend and you have no clue as to what we were talking about or what's going on."

He turned away, not being able to cope with her look of horror at his scolding.

"Martha," Jake began, "I'm not your enemy. I know you know more than you're letting on. Please, let's do this together, or at least tell me what you know so I have some idea of what I'm dealing with."

Before Martha could utter a word, Marion interrupted: "Yes, why don't you? Tell Jake what you know about his sister's death; tell him what you are."

"Why do you always have to interfere," Martha yelled at her. "Just because you were such a crap mum to Amy, you think you can lay all the blame for your family's problems on me!"

"How dare you?" Marion shouted back. "You're the one who used my daughter; now you think you can take advantage of my son as well …"

"Hey, hang on a minute," Jake told her. "Martha isn't using me; I told you I'm an adult, you can't presume to run my life. I'm the one who asked Martha for a roof over my head; I'm the one who wanted to seduce her and I'm the one trying to win her trust. I don't need you waltzing in here, attempting to take over as if I'm still a five-year-old."

Jake paused. He glanced from one woman to the other. Although he was surprised to see Martha looking the quieter of the two, he knew her temper could explode at any moment with his mum clearly trying to goad her into an argument.

"Why can't you two just be friends?" He asked. "You're both important people in my life; I have no intention of changing that," Jake continued, looking pointedly at his mum. "Life would be much less complicated if you could at least try to get along."

"You don't know what you're asking," Marion implored. "I can't accept the person I know is responsible for your sister's death in our lives. She's dangerous. The sooner you realise that, the better."

"After all this time, why can't you just accept Amy died as a result of a terrible accident? You've got to let her rest in peace and get on with the rest of your life." Jake told her, not satisfied with the lack of strength behind his words.

Marion felt her cheeks burning. "Why can't you be honest with him?" She snapped at Martha. "You were more than happy to tell me what really happened on that hillside. She's evil, Jake," Marion continued, glancing back at her son. "I can see how you'd fall for her, but what you see in her, is not the truth."

Martha gave a small laugh.

"What's that supposed to mean?" Jake demanded.

"She was there, with your sister, when she died. Martha didn't just happen to turn up at your school after Amy died; she was already there."

Jake frowned, looking from his mum to Martha. His head was reeling but the soreness in his arm had faded by comparison, after listening to his mum's tirade. He shook his head slowly. "Whatever happened back then, we can't change. All I do know is that there is something out there, in those woods," he added, pointing in the general direction.

"Mum, I need Martha's help. I will deal with whatever she chooses to tell me, or not, about Amy, but for now, for my sake, can't you just drop this and let me deal with what's happening here in my own way. There are things which you haven't given me a chance to tell you about yet, things which might help you to deal with what occurred ten years ago."

Jake turned to stand between the two women, watching them both carefully. "I need you to accept a truce. Fine, if you can't be friends, that's not important right now. What is important, is that we work together to find out what is causing these deaths in the woods and whether there's any way of stopping it from continuing."

Marion pulled a look of distaste and turned away as if suddenly interested in looking out of the window.

Jake turned his attention fully back to Martha. He took her hand up in his. "I'm sorry," he began, "if I've made a mess of things; I can't pretend to understand this situation, or to be any good at dealing with it. Fine, I understand if you say you can't trust me. I want to change that and will do everything I can to prove myself to you. I don't know what's going on here, or in the woods. Whatever you know though, I want you to tell me and I promise I won't judge you."

Marion laughed, turning to face them and beginning to speak again.

"Just butt out, Mum, please," Jake told her, before she could mutter a single syllable. "This is between Martha and me."

Marion shrugged and watched them, biting her lip.

Martha looked at her with a vague appearance of superiority, which wasn't lost on Jake, but he was desperate to put a stop to their petty bickering.

"If I tell you what you want to know," Martha began slowly, "I know you'll hate me."

"I'll never hate you," Jake told her.

Marion couldn't prevent the laugh of disgust escaping from her mouth.

Martha glanced from mother to son. "You need to go with your mum," she told Jake. "She's right, no good can come of your being here; in fact, you are putting yourself in unnecessary danger the longer you remain."

Martha held up her hand as Jake tried to respond. "Just go, Jake. If Amy meant anything to you, if I mean anything to you, you need to leave this village. Yes, there's evil here and it is far beyond anything you could ever conquer."

Jake felt a pain in the pit of his stomach. He was quickly realising he wouldn't like the sound of the truth, if these two ever let him anywhere near it, but he was determined not to give up. After coming this far, he wanted to know what was lurking out there.

"I'm not about to give up," he told Martha. "Either you can tell me what you know, thereby helping me, or, I'll go it alone and take my chances."

They stood in silence. The sound of a lorry lurching up over the top of the hill, came from the direction of the road. Jake tried to wait patiently, both wanting Martha to speak to him, yet afraid of what he might hear.

It was Marion who broke the silence. "Martha, I know I've perhaps, not always been fair to you, despite what you told me. I can never forget what happened and I'm not asking you to forgive me. However, for Jake's sake, I'm willing to put my personal feelings aside, if it means we can help Jake and keep him safe. I couldn't bear to lose him as well."

Jake gave his mum a small smile, knowing how much effort her little speech must have taken. He looked back at Martha. She was looking at the floor, rubbing at an invisible mark with her toes.

At length, she lifted her head, gave a cursory glance in Marion's direction, before fixing her eyes on Jake.

"You can't do this, Jake. You cannot win. Your priest was right; you're trying to deal with something which is centuries old and has had all that time to increase in strength, becoming more powerful and less discriminate."

Wishing to keep her talking, Jake asked: "What is out there?"

Martha sighed. "Let's go and sit down."

They followed her into the sitting room. Marion gazed at the décor before sitting in the corner of the sofa. Jake sat in his usual armchair, whilst Martha took a commanding position in the centre of the sofa.

"The priest was correct about the woman tied to the tree when the castle stood. However, the tree had been there for hundreds of years before that time. It was a birch tree; they have been associated with death for as long as anyone can remember. People are aware of its links with new life and fertility, but its role as a threshold between this world and the next, tends to be conveniently forgotten. The tree's history goes back to a time when people believed in spirits and folklore was rife."

Receiving no response or questions from her audience, Martha continued her tale: "No one is exactly sure when the tree was first possessed by a spirit. These things are only discovered once the spirit is in situ and beginning to set to work. But, long before then, women came to the woods to ask the Sleeper in the birch to bless them with the gift of children."

"One woman who visited the tree, came often; she longed for children but remained unmarried. In fact, she found comfort from the face she saw in the bark. Fearing she would die childless, eventually she told the tree she was prepared to do anything in order to become a mother, even to become part of the tree itself, she thought, might mean she would be blessed with children; she believed the tree was inhabited by the soul of the Sleeper she saw there, and he might provide her with her own offspring. The tree refused all her requests, instead asking her to be patient."

"However, the tree was riddled with a fungus known as Witches' Broom. Having heard her plea to the tree, the evil inside the fungus told the woman, if she hung herself from a branch of the tree, she would gain immortality and therefore more time in which to mother children. It also promised her she would bear the children of the mystical tree itself."

"In her desperation, the lonely woman was easily persuaded and one night killed herself by tying a rope around her neck and hanging her body from a branch of the birch."

"Her corpse remained undisturbed and the fungus slowly consumed her, entwining her body with that of the tree and filling her with its own evil. Over time, it became impossible to see her. The woman's spirit was angry that she had been tricked; she bore no children and her immortality was useless to her as she was trapped inside the tree. She became bitter. Vowing to punish others as she had been herself, yet still holding on to the wish to have children of her own, she set about enticing those who came to the tree as she had once been fooled."

Jake scowled at his mum as she sighed heavily. He was quite aware of how fantastic Martha's tale sounded, yet he didn't want her to stop talking. Having the impression now that she was willing to share her knowledge with them, he didn't want her to become silent again. He focused his attention back on Martha who looked as if she was seeing the story unfolding before her as she spoke.

"As the woman gained more victims for the evil spirit inside her and the tree, girls who were willing to give themselves up to the birch in exchange for fertility, so her strength increased until it was she who controlled the tree. The Sleeper no longer had the appearance of a beautiful spirit, instead it appeared decrepit and evil. This led women to begin staying away from the tree, choosing to seek out other birches instead. The woman realised she needed to become more cunning in luring her victims."

Martha paused, glancing at them both. "Now we come to your priest's part of the story," she explained.

"By the time the witch from the castle was tied to the tree for the night before her trial, the spirit inside it was so strong that the body was consumed within one night. However, just like all those who had gone before her, she soon longed for her freedom again. But people avoided the tree, tales spread about this birch yet no one would go close enough to it to destroy it. The person whose soul was contained within the birch became more adept at enticing their next victim in order to regain their own freedom."

"As the old man told you," Martha directed herself towards Jake, "with what strength the tree had, it would release its victim from the hold of the evil possessing it, whenever its occupant presented it with a new body. The evil spirit didn't care how a new victim was claimed, as long as it was female."

The room fell silent. Jake knew what he wanted to know, yet was loathe to ask the question. He glanced at his mum. She was clearly finding it difficult to reconcile herself to being in such close proximity with Martha; her face contorted with a mixture of pain and interest.

"You believe all this?" He asked at length.

Martha looked down at her hands twisting in her lap. "It's safest to listen to such tales. Even if it isn't all true, there will be some truth which is meant to be heeded."

"And you?" Jake asked Marion. "What do you think?"

Marion looked from her son and then to Martha before she replied. "It sounds like a fairy tale to me. However, when your sister died, I did discover some strange things had occurred, which Martha now seems unwilling to acknowledge."

Jake held his breath. After getting these two women in the same room without a fuss, he didn't want it to break down now. However, Martha remained silent as Marion continued.

"There has to be some explanation for the deaths in the woods, and for girls seeming to come back to life." Her eyes remained fixed on Martha as she spoke.

"You think some of it could be true?" Jake asked.

Marion shrugged. "You have to ask her about that," she replied, pointing at Martha dismissively.

"I've seen a girl in the village who looks exactly like Amy; she was in the woods too," Jake spoke quickly.

Marion's attention turned to her son. "Amy? Did you speak to her?"

He glanced nervously at Martha who, for the first time, appeared to be interested in their conversation.

"Her name's Amelia; I spoke to her but she didn't show any signs of recognising me."

Marion jumped up from her seat. "We've got to find her," she stated, stepping towards the door.

"Hang on, Mum," Jake sighed.

"It could be your sister," Marion snapped.

"She didn't know me," Jake told her.

Marion turned back and looked at Martha. Begrudgingly, she addressed herself to the younger woman. "Could it be Amy?"

For the first time since he'd known her, Jake was surprised to see Martha looking uncertain of herself.

Martha chewed her lip. Her gaze was focused on the window as though she was deciding what to say, if anything. Eventually, she turned her attention to Marion.

"It's possible," she replied simply. "But, you should be aware, not everyone has any recollection of their previous existence. It could be Amy, but if she didn't recognise Jake, it's likely she has no recall to her past."

"Or, she's not Amy at all?" Jake suggested. "That's got to be a possibility too."

Neither woman took any notice of him. Jake looked worryingly at his mum. The last thing he wanted was for her to build her hopes up of being reunited with her daughter.

Marion turned to her son. "You're the one who mentioned this girl. When did you first see her?"

Jake shifted his weight. "In the woods, by a fallen tree; it was the day they found the girl's body."

For a moment, he paused, hand half-raised. "Oh my god!" He suddenly blurted.

Martha and Marion stared at him.

"When the police were interviewing me, they told me Amelia had reported seeing me where they had found the dead girl. Isn't it a bit of a coincidence that's where she was? How could she have known that's where the body was discovered to tell the police where I was, unless she knew the body was there herself?"

Jake and Marion looked expectantly at Martha. She stood up and walked to the window, her eyes gazing blindly at the outside world.

"It could be a coincidence," Martha muttered.

"You know that's not the case," Marion told her. "Have you seen her too?"

Without facing them, Martha replied: "No."

Jake's mind was racing. This was a link. A first step towards linking Reverend Jackson's tale to what Martha had told them. No one would believe them, of course, particularly as Amelia hadn't known him from Adam. But if the story was true, then it meant his sister had somehow been responsible for the death of this new victim. He shivered. Jake tried to force himself to ignore that part as a vision of his sister came into his head with her wielding a heavy branch over the figure of a small girl.

He gazed up at Martha. What could they do with this information? He wondered. Was there any way they could stop the pattern of deaths continuing?

"Martha?" He hazarded.

Slowly, she turned to face him.

Jake was startled by the look of sadness on her face. He'd never seen such vulnerability in her. "What can we do?"

She glanced down before looking back at him a little more confidently. "Nothing. I told you, go home, both of you." Martha threw a brief look at Marion. "This has been going on for hundreds of years and will probably continue to do so for hundreds more. You can't stop it; it's much too powerful. Besides, …"

Jake watched her as she faced the window again. "Besides what?" He prompted her.

"You don't know what it might do to the girls who have been lucky enough to escape from it."

Jake frowned and glanced at his mum. She shrugged. They waited for Martha to continue.

"If the girl you saw is Amy," Martha said eventually, "and you try to destroy the tree, you have no way of knowing whether she would survive."

"What do you mean?" Jake asked. "How can the tree still have any influence on her when she's living her new life away from it?"

Martha shrugged and turned to face them. "I don't know," she replied. "And that's the problem. We have no way of knowing if the tree, or what's inside it, still has any influence. After all, if you think about it, it's not natural for a life to be regained; the force inside the tree lets it happen when a new corpse is given to it. Once the girl escapes, I can't tell you whether she is beholden to the tree any longer. In destroying it, you could kill her and all the other girls who have been expelled too."

"And you know all this because ..." Marion drawled.

Jake glanced at his mum. "Shut up!"

A heavy silence hung in the air between them. It had been a long time since Jake had seen his mum looking this animated, yet her motivation appeared to be balanced precariously on seeing Martha in the unfamiliar position of seeming to be vulnerable. It wasn't a trait he could admire, even though it had his curiosity piqued.

There was an uneasy stand-off. Jake had never noticed the sound of a clock ticking somewhere in the room before now but it suddenly seemed deafening.

Eventually, Martha looked up from her hands. "Your mum's right, Jake," she whispered. "I was there when Amy died. I am responsible for your sister's death."

Before he could process her words, or even consider responding, Jake watched in shock as Marion launched herself at Martha with the fury she had kept suppressed inside her for the previous ten years.

Seeing his mother's fists clutching at Martha's long hair and showering her with abuse, Jake suddenly found his feet and dragged his mum backwards.

Words hurled themselves relentlessly at the screaming girl. Both women's faces were red, yet Martha made no effort to defend herself, allowing Marion's fists and curses to rain down upon her.

Jake was panting with the effort of restraining his mum, but held onto her waist until she, eventually, became quieter. Sitting between the two women, Jake turned his attention to Martha. "Tell me what happened," he begged.

Slowly, Martha's hands straightened her tousled hair. Jake noticed the shakiness of her fingers and how the colour had faded quickly from her face. He wasn't sure how he felt, but he knew he needed to hear her own account of what had happened to his sister.

Martha's eyes remained fixed on her lap as she began to finally speak: "I was a child when I came to the tree. It was a good hiding place. Things weren't great at home, my father hated me; he blamed me for my mother's death. She died when I was born," Martha explained. "I think if she'd survived my birth, my whole life would have been completely different."

"I felt sorry for him, at first. He missed my mother and was left with a crying child and no wife. He tried his best, but he didn't have a clue how to raise a daughter. Even though his own mother came to live with us, she'd only had sons herself. I probably wasn't the easiest girl to live with; I was a bit wild. Maybe it was my own way of dealing with my mother's death and the guilt I was showered with."

"The odd slap, I could cope with, deserved even. However, when my grandmother died, Dad managed to become even more difficult to please. He picked holes in everything I did or said. My backside was probably permanently red from the beatings he told me I deserved. I spent less and less time at home, anything to avoid being in the same place as him. Gradually I came to hate him; he seemed to enjoy hurting me. When I was smaller, it was easy for him to make me cry. I suppose as I got older, and more defiant, he had to try harder as I became more determined not to let him see how much he could hurt me."

Jake wanted to reassure her, tell her it was okay, despite what she'd done. Yet, he couldn't bring himself to open his mouth, or reach out to her. Martha was in a world of her own. He found it hard to imagine she'd ever spoken these words aloud to anyone. He wanted to turn and look at his mum, but he was mesmerised by Martha.

"I stayed away for longer and longer periods. I found the woods were a comfort; there was always things to see, food to scavenge. It was peaceful, a place where I didn't feel scared. I used to tell myself my mother could see me and was watching me from heaven; I felt closer to her in those woods, between our house and the place her body was laid to rest."

"One day, I'd gone home to change my clothes and get something a bit more substantial to eat. I thought my father would be out at work, but it was like he was waiting for me. I was barely through the door when he slammed it shut and shoved me into the wall. If I'd known he was there, I might have been more able to protect myself, but I was winded when I hit the wall. I was on the floor and his feet were kicking into me before I even realised it was him. I begged him to stop, I promised I'd leave and never come back but he didn't want to hear me. My words fell on deaf ears; he was wild with anger and lashed out until I could no longer speak. I was only nine years old."

Martha paused. After a few moments, she continued, her voice little more than a whisper: "I think he thought he'd killed me. Suddenly he stopped. I daren't move; I didn't know if I could move, every part of my body seemed to be screaming in agony. I heard the door slam and his footsteps disappeared. I don't know how long I lay there. Knowing I had to get out of that cottage before he came back and finished off the job, I slowly managed to stand up and leave. The forest was the place I thought of to go to. I've no idea how I got myself there but I did. It was beginning to get dark and all I wanted to do was to sleep. I found a fallen tree and crawled underneath it; there was a bigger space than I had imagined and the ground was covered in pine needles and leaves. It was the softest bed I had ever known."

"As I fell asleep, I was sure I heard a woman's voice, singing. I told myself it was my mother, that she'd come to comfort me and protect me. I soon slept."

Martha raised her hands to her face and covered her eyes. She made no sound as Jake watched her. He'd always supposed she'd not had the happiest of childhoods; Martha had never spoken about her life before she'd come to the village, and Jake had never thought to ask her about it, deciding she would tell him what she wanted him to know.

But hearing her story now, the pain she'd experienced was evident. Despite what she'd said about Amy, Jake found it impossible to feel anything other than pity for her.

"It was like a dream." Martha's hands dropped back to her lap as she began speaking again. "Instead of a tree, I could believe I was lying with my mother; I even felt her arms wrapped around me. I didn't want to leave, for the first time in my life, I felt as though I was loved and someone was holding me close to them because it was what they wanted. I don't know how much time passed, all I knew was that I couldn't go back home and I had nowhere else to go. Death wasn't frightening; it was a relief. There was no more pain, no cold or hunger; in fact, I felt warmer and more content in that state than I'd experienced before, or since."

"So why did you have to hurt Amy?" Marion's voice cut through the air like a knife, accusation and anger fuelling her question.

Martha's eyes remained fixed on her lap but her body clearly flinched at the sound of Marion's words.

"It wasn't my choice. I can only presume the tree no longer wanted me; the evil which lurks there needed a new victim. Amy's dog disturbed the ground and when she appeared, events were set in motion which couldn't be stopped."

"You're telling us you had no power to stop yourself pushing my daughter to her death?" Marion asked incredulously.

"I wasn't the one in control," Martha spat. "Amy became the next victim as soon as she dragged her dog back from the tree. She was perfect: young, innocent and too trusting. The first I knew about what was happening was when your daughter rushed into me when I suddenly found myself forced out from under the tree and was standing, minding my own business, on a path in the woods. Words came out of my mouth which I didn't speak. It was like I was possessed and my body moved and my mouth spoke without me knowing what was going to happen next."

"And you expect us to believe you?" Marion snapped, pulling herself forward.

Martha continued as before. "I don't need you to believe me. All I can do is tell you what happened and what I know. You believe what you want."

"Jake?"

Jake glanced at his mum as she muttered his name. He had no idea what was true. As much as he wanted to try and stop anyone else having to go through what he and his mum did, he knew this tale was getting more and more difficult to share with anyone else.

"When Amy fell, all I knew was how much comfort I had found under the tree when I had gone there myself to die. It was the only place I could think of for her. I didn't know much about Amy's home life then, only that she spent as much time in those woods as I once had. I assumed her situation wasn't that different to what mine had been," Martha confessed.

"But it wasn't like that!" Marion screamed.

Slowly Martha turned to face them. "I didn't know that. Being able to give Amy the experience I had found such comfort in was like being able to share a gift with her. It wasn't until she laid at the foot of the hill that I discovered I could control my own body. It could have been anyone's hand which pushed her from the peak; yes, I know it was mine, but it wasn't, if you know what I mean. I found myself back inside my body when Amy opened her eyes after her fall. As her strength weakened, mine grew. Somehow, I helped her to get to the tree and watched her as she fell asleep underneath it; she even smiled. When her body was recovered and taken away, her spirit remained there quite happily. I can't tell you when or if Amy is alive again, all I can say is that I went from seeing her fall asleep for the last time under the tree, to finding myself wandering the streets of Sheffield more than thirty years after I had died."

Jake turned his attention from Martha to look at his mum. Her face was blotchy and she was struggling to find something to say.

"I think we're all exhausted," he said slowly. "There's no point in anyone getting angry or upset now. I'm certain the girl who calls herself Amelia is my sister. From what Martha's said, she may not be aware of that. We can't go frightening her with this. I think we need to take a break now and think about how to move forward."

Marion gave him a cursory glance, stood up and walked across the room to the window.

"Where are you staying?" Jake asked her.

"At a hotel in the city," she replied as she gazed out of the window.

"Do you want me to call you a taxi?"

"No, Jake," she replied quickly. "I'll get a bus. What are you going to do now?"

He glanced at Martha. Her attention was focused back on her hands. He nudged her gently. "What do you want me to do?" Jake asked her.

"I need some time alone," Martha replied without looking at him.

Jake nodded and sighed. "I'll catch the bus with you," he told Marion. "But I'm going back to see Reverend Jackson, see if he has anything further to say."

"I'll go with you," Marion stated.

"No," Jake said emphatically. "He's an old man; he doesn't need hounding from both of us. Besides, he's met me before, it'll be easier if I go alone."

They let themselves out of the house, with Jake telling Martha he'd be back later to check she was okay. Without waiting for a response, he followed his mum to the road, where they took the long route to the village along the road, not wishing to cut through the woods.

Neither of them spoke. They arrived at the bus stop as a bus pulled up and Jake was the first to alight as the vehicle reached the outskirts of the city.

As he walked to the old people's home, he knew he should have made more of an effort to say something to his mum. But his head was swimming with information he was finding difficult to digest, and he wasn't sure his mum was ready to have a conversation about reincarnation or evil spirits. So, he'd promised her he would head to her hotel once he'd spoken to the priest again.

It felt odd being back at the home; Jake hadn't expected to ever have the need to return again. However, he hoped the old man might be able to offer some ideas on how to proceed as he was the only person Jake knew who clearly believed in the strange stories relating to the tree, and what was happening in the woods.

The entrance hall was quiet and Jake waited patiently for someone to come to the reception desk. Eventually the smiling face of a woman he'd never seen before, asked how she could help him.

"I've come to see Reverend Jackson," Jake explained. "I've been a couple of times and, as I was passing, thought I'd pop in for a chat."

The woman looked at him apologetically. "I'm really very sorry," she began, "but, Reverend Jackson died yesterday."

Jake was unable to hide the shock from his face.

"I'm so sorry you had to find out like this," she added quickly. "Are you family? Can I get you anything? A glass of water, perhaps?"

Jake shook his head. "No, thank you," he muttered as he stepped away from the desk.

"It was a shock to us all," the woman added. "So very unexpected."

Trying to keep his breathing steady, Jake turned away and headed out through the door into the fresh, cool air. Stumbling slightly as he made his way back down the driveway, Jake pictured the old man as he'd last seen him. It was difficult to believe he was dead. That dreadful word seemed to be haunting him; it was everywhere.

At the main road, Jake hesitated. What could he do now? He'd promised he'd go straight to his mum's hotel but his head was reeling. What could he say to her? No, he needed time to think, time to decide what to do next. Looking up, Jake saw a Bradfield bus approaching. Without pausing, Jake raced across the road, narrowly avoiding a cyclist who yelled a stream of expletives at him in his wake.

Out of breath, Jake dropped onto an empty seat in the bus and rested his head against the window. He really didn't have a clue where he was going or what to do, but he knew he couldn't do nothing.

Chapter 8

It was the second time he'd seen her, apparently, hanging around the bus stop. This time though, as Jake stepped off the bus, it was Amelia who moved hesitantly towards him. Not wishing to scare her off, Jake waited patiently, pretending to check his phone.

"I know you, don't I?" her voice was quiet; she sounded frightened.

Jake nodded, unsure what to say.

"I keep having these dreams," Amelia continued. "You're always there. I know I'm fostered; I don't live with my real family," she explained. "But in the dreams, I'm with you and a different mum."

She lowered her head. Jake wasn't sure what she expected from him. He was hardly in a position to make things any clearer for her, but at least this time, she wasn't hurrying to get away from him.

"Why do you think you're having these dreams?" he asked. "Has anything happened recently, which could have triggered them?"

Amelia looked back at him, her eyes just like Amy's; it made Jake's heart skip a beat.

"I don't think so, that girl was killed, and obviously I saw you in the woods."

"You don't seem scared of me any more," Jake told her.

Amelia shrugged. "I just get the idea I don't need to be frightened of you. Should I be?"

For a moment Jake wondered whether she was toying with him as a smile seemed to play around the corner of her mouth.

"I'm not sure what you want me to say," Jake told her. He glanced along the quiet road, feeling vulnerable alone with this teenage girl, especially after his questioning by the police.

"Who are you? Why do I think I know you?"

Jake stubbed out an imaginary cigarette with his foot. When he looked back at Amelia, she was watching him, waiting.

He took a deep breath. "I lived in this village as a boy, with my mum and sister, Amy, as I told you before. Amy died in an accident, she fell from a hilltop but they found her body in the woods, probably where we first bumped into each other."

"I'm sorry," Amelia mumbled as he paused.

"Thanks, it was a long time ago, ten years. You look really like her, it's why it threw me, the first time I saw you; I thought you were Amy."

"I'm fifteen too," Amelia said slowly.

"I don't know why you're having those dreams. I don't mean you any harm, I promise," Jake said. "I came back because I wanted to see if the place had changed. I'd been having dreams about Amy so it was kind of weird to see you when I got here."

"So, you don't actually think I am Amy?" She looked at him innocently, although Jake felt the weight in the question.

"That would be impossible, wouldn't it?" he replied.

She gave a small laugh. "I s'pose so." Amelia gave him a final cursory glance, waved her hand and headed up the hill.

Jake watched her retreating figure: the black leather jacket looked worn and heavy and her Dr Marten boots looked about three sizes too large for her feet. She looked like a girl lost in her own body, Jake decided. He wanted to run after her and tell her what he knew about the tree and its story, but he held himself back. She really would think he was a nutter and he couldn't afford for her to go running back to the police about him.

Once Amelia had disappeared from his view, Jake turned and headed to the entrance of the woods; he wanted to see whether he would be able to find his way back to the tree.

Stepping over the stile by the roadside was like moving through a portal. On the road, the daylight wasn't exactly bright but the day was still light and Jake felt warm enough in just short sleeves; birdsong and the breeze created enough sound, along with the occasional passing vehicle to show that all was right with the world.

However, as soon as Jake found himself inside the boundary of the woodland, the trees managed to shut out a lot of the daylight, despite being deplete of leaves. The silence was eerie and he rubbed his hands along his goose-bump covered arms. Jake tried to force a laugh out of himself, annoyed for getting spooked this quickly and easily. He knew his imagination was working on overtime and tried, in vain, to calm his breathing.

His upward climb was slow but steady. The single footpath was wide and clear of debris making walking easy. It was unsurprising to feel someone was watching him; Jake resisted the urge to look over his shoulder and tried not to jump whenever the sound of a twig snapping, or rustling from the undergrowth, came to his ears.

However, the flash of red, darting across his path, brought Jake suddenly to a halt. He swallowed. Determinedly, he began walking again, finding it impossible now to think of anything other than the tale of the birch tree.

As Jake slowed, coming to a fork in the path, he peered in both directions. He didn't like being indecisive, feeling he needed to keep moving. Suddenly, aware of a movement on the path to his right, Jake swallowed the cry which threatened to pour from his mouth as he stared at the small girl standing before him.

It was like being thrust back in time as he watched her. Her appearance was exactly like his first view of Martha when she'd turned up for her first day at his school in the village. This girl though, wore a bright, red cloak, a tartan skirt showed beneath it and her brown, leather boots were caked in mud.

Confidently she held his gaze as they stared silently at each other.

"Martha?" Jake muttered eventually.

She simply watched him, a glimmer of laughter seemed to lurk at the corner of her dark eyes.

Annoyed with himself for showing his shock, Jake strode forward, brushing past her as he chose to take that way onwards. Getting some distance between him and the girl, Jake risked a backward glance; there was no longer any sign of her.

He'd only gone a short distance when the sound of creaking wood came to Jake's ears. Jumping back quickly as he realised the noise was perilously close, he ran his hands through his hair as a heavy bough, dropped onto the path just a few feet in front of him.

Glancing round quickly, Jake drew in a deep breath as he looked straight into the eyes of his sister. She was standing so close, Jake could feel the cold exhalation of breath from between her lips. Wearing her familiar jeans and a shirt he easily recalled from all those years before, Jake could only stare at the apparition.

He knew he was terrified, but his curiosity was piqued too. How could Amy be here? Like the previous girl, Amy simply stared at him, a quiet look of amusement poorly shielded from him.

"Amy?" Jake whispered as he reached out to touch her.

His hand reached the thin fabric of her shirt. His movement appeared abhorrent to her as she leapt back as though he'd struck her violently.

Jake held up his hands in apology. "I'm sorry; I just can't believe it's you."

Something suddenly appeared to startle her. Amy's head spun round as she looked at something in the distance which was lost on Jake. All at once, she took off, running through the trees before Jake could even decide whether to follow her.

Once again alone, he took a hesitant step forward before resuming his way along the path. Barely more than a few paces further, Jake stopped abruptly again as he saw another figure in his way. It was the girl who had gone missing; the girl he'd been questioned over by the police.

Just like the other two, she simply stared at him, not moving.

"It's okay," Jake said quietly as he took a step towards her. She looked so real, alive even, despite knowing her dead body had been found by the police. Was he looking at a ghost? Jake wondered. Is that what he'd seen before, with Amy and Martha?

Feeling the fear rising inside his chest, Jake glanced around him. Every direction he looked in, the figure of a girl stood silently watching him. Their eyes felt like they were boring holes into his body. Where could they all have come from? There must be nearly a hundred of them, Jake decided, all around him, within touching distance and far into the woods too.

Without thinking, Jake rushed forward, his shoulder knocking heavily into the small girl who had stood in his path. It was like hitting a rock as he ran past her; she barely reacted. Dodging other figures, Jake raced on, not thinking now about where he was heading.

He stopped. His chest was hurting from the effort of running. Leaning against the trunk of a tree, Jake paused, panting heavily. As he began to regain his breath, Jake opened his eyes and looked around him. There were no girls any longer but a soft breeze was beginning, whipping up leaves from the ground so that they swirled in the air, dancing and leaping, quickly increasing in their numbers. The breeze became stronger, turning into a torrent of wind, sweeping between the trees and moaning as it twisted and turned.

Jake found himself gripping the bark beneath his fingers. He squinted as he looked about him, protecting his eyes from the darting leaves which struck his face at intervals.

The air was filled with creaking branches straining under the strength of the wind which, itself, screamed as it swept between the trees around him. Aware of the danger from falling branches and trees, Jake took a deep breath and staggered onwards, pausing as he reached each tree along the path.

Then, as he reached out, the wind suddenly ceased and Jake fell forward, landing heavily on the ground and his shoulder hitting an obstacle which lay in his way.

Groaning, as he slowly pulled himself up, Jake realised he was leaning against a fallen tree trunk. Shocked, he drew back quickly as though the contact had burnt him.

Forcing himself to keep breathing, Jake studied the trunk. It looked as though it had rested in this position for a long time, a deep groove around the rim, showed it had settled deeply into the surrounding dirt.

The bark looked dry. Each end of the long trunk was roughly severed. Slowly Jake stood up, his legs shaking so that he couldn't help but lean against the tree for support. As he rested his hands on the top of the fallen tree, Jake looked in amazement at the small twig, sprouting close to his fingers. There was a tiny, green shoot at the tip. Gingerly, Jake reached out and touched the new, folded leaf. He peered down at it; there could be no doubt: this was a living leaf.

Curiosity drove Jake to walk around the trunk. Both ends were definitely detached from the ground and as he moved to the far side of the trunk, Jake could see more young shoots flourishing on this, apparently, dead corpse of a tree.

He broke off a section of bark. The wood beneath was pale. Jake rapped his knuckles against the trunk; the sound was hollow. This must be the one, he told himself as he dropped to his knees. Peering at the underside of the tree, he brushed aside dead leaves from the ground until a hollow was visible, disappearing below the tree like a giant rabbit hole.

Kneeling back up on his haunches, Jake looked at the area around him. Yes, he thought, I know this place; this is it. Relief was mixed with fear. What happens now? Jake hadn't considered what he'd do if he found the tree again. Had he expected a solution to come to him out of the ether? The memory of his last visit to this site made him hesitate to reach beneath the tree. Jake hauled himself to his feet and gently rested himself against the trunk.

As he looked down into the abyss, Jake became aware of an acrid odour invading his nostrils. The smell slowly increased until it made him retch. Standing upright again, Jake turned his back to the trunk, gasping at the fresher air to clear his lungs.

Something pulling at the leg of his jeans made Jake glance down: nothing. The sound of laughter came to his ears: childlike, taunting. His eyes scanned his surroundings, looking for the source of the noise but the girls were nowhere to be seen. Telling himself it was fanciful, the work of some ancient spirit, helped Jake to quell his growing fear. Whatever lurked in the tree was playing with him, trying to scare him with a phantom display which could fit into any horror novel.

As he began coughing, Jake realised the smell had returned, even more over-powering than before. He turned back towards the trunk. A faint mist was swirling around the hollow. Whilst Jake stared at the increasing vapour, a pair of hands appeared from beneath the tree.

Aghast, Jake watched the bony fingers grasp at the ground. Long, thin nails, almost claw-like, reached from the finger tips, stretching upwards. As the hands extended outwards, narrow, scab-covered arms were revealed. The grey skin appeared, painfully thin, barely covering the bones and muscles visible below.

The sight was abhorrent, yet Jake was unable to drag his eyes from this apparition. He stepped backwards to keep out of the reach of this disgusting creature which was slowly revealing itself to him.

Unaware of the stone beneath his foot, it wasn't until he found himself falling backwards that Jake felt the twist of his ankle. Hands frantically grasping at the air, he was unable to prevent himself from hitting the ground, the impact sucking the breath out of him sharply.

His feet kicking hurriedly at the ground, Jake heard himself cry out with the pain which shot through his ankle. He cursed aloud as the phantom fingers just missed the touch of his boot as he dragged himself backwards.

Shaking, Jake watched as the top of a head now appeared between the two arms as the monstrosity pulled itself from beneath the trunk. Dark tendrils of hair showed, grey flesh formed a wide forehead as two empty eye sockets looked out from a skeletal face. A gap, which might have once been a nose, lay above the mouth framed by blackened lips.

Somehow, Jake knew he was looking at the spectre of a woman. With the head and arms now visible, the rest of the body was dragged from her resting place.

The long, bony corpse seemed to stretch endlessly up into air in front of Jake. Despite the lack of eyeballs, she appeared to watch him as she rose to her dizzying full height.

Jake estimated she stood at least eight, if not nine, feet tall. Swaying on a pair of feet, supported by thin, dirt-covered legs which disappeared beneath a ragged, brownish garment which had once, presumably, been a dress. The creature paused.

Reminding himself to keep breathing, Jake waited, remaining still on the ground.

Two arms reached out towards him: sharp talons swiped the air just inches from Jake's face. He pulled back in disgust as his heels dug into the earth for some leverage. Clods of soil flew up, yet the creature didn't hesitate. A hand lashed out towards Jake's shoulder; he ducked to the side, but not without a tear appearing in the sleeve of his shirt.

Rolling his body over, Jake started crawling away from the thing looming above him. Desperately his hands reached through the leaves and soil, clutching at anything he could grasp to pull himself out of harm's way.

In an instant, Jake felt himself sucked up into the air. Pain tore across his back as he gazed helplessly down at the retreating ground beneath him. The creature held what was left of his shirt between its skeletal fingers; Jake was very aware of each individual gash which had been ripped into the flesh on his back.

Lile a puppet, he was suspended, slowly being turned by his captor as the remains of the creature's face inspected its prey.

A wide grin opened on the mouth of the face, its eyes screwed themselves up as it looked into Jake's face. He could feel the putrid odour emanating from its whole being: the smell of pure evil.

Jake felt his eyelids flickering as the scent threatened to suffocate him. What contents he had remaining in his stomach suddenly hurled themselves up and the vomit splattered to the ground.

In an instant Jake found himself plummeting earthwards as his body was abruptly dropped. He groaned at the thud but mustered the energy to turn himself onto his back so he could see what might come next.

The pain from his back was excruciating, yet he fought to remain conscious, focusing on the actions of his captor.

A foot, heavy in spite of its lack of any substance, was placed on Jake's chest, pinning him down. Although loath to touch it, Jake wrapped his fingers around the base of the giant foot, trying to force the pressure off his body.

As he pushed up, so the pressure downwards seemed to increase. Jake knew if he let go, his torso would be easily crushed. He tried to wriggle his body free but the single foot was enough to hold him firmly in place with apparent little effort.

"What do you want from me?" Jake gasped.

In response, Jake felt the pressure on his chest begin to increase, very gradually, but without doubt, bit by bit, the weight on his body was building. Jake quickly realised, if he did nothing, his ribs would crack, one by one, until his chest was crushed.

A sharp snap accompanied an excruciating pain as Jake knew his first rib had collapsed. Tears of frustration stung his eyes as the extent of his helplessness, at the mercy of this monster, became clear. He was going to die here, in the same place his sister had all those years ago. His mum would be mourning the death of her second child at the hands of the same perpetrator.

The sound of a second crack ripped through Jake's body. His breath became raspy as each breath drew a searing agony through his torso. His eyelids fluttered as he struggled to remain conscious. Jake's view of the creature towering over him blurred in and out of sight.

Suddenly, a scream split the air in two. The pressure on his chest was momentarily eased. Aware enough to take advantage of the change in his situation, Jake flung himself on his side and pulled himself free from the aim of the giant foot which then thundered onto the ground where he had just laid.

The more Jake gasped for air, the stronger the hurt which wracked his body. Somehow, he dragged himself along the muddy ground. A voice came to his ears as an almighty yell of fury poured from the creature's mouth sending a rancid vapour in Jake's direction.

The words were unidentifiable in his confusion but Jake sensed the urgency as he felt a grip on his shoulder. With a huge effort, Jake held onto the hand which held him as he slowly edged himself backwards. As another animalistic roar came from the spectre, it acted as a momentum for Jake to speed up his escape, ignoring the pain and staggering blindly forward.

Tumbling downhill and heaving his weary body ever forwards, Jake gradually became aware of his companion. The small hand, with nails painted black, which held his arm, belonged to Amelia.

Her face was painted with fear, yet Jake couldn't help but admire her bravery in helping him. He tried to pull his mouth into a smile, although he imagined it probably had the appearance of a pained grimace.

"Thank you," Jake mouthed silently as they reached the narrow bridge.

Amelia released her hold on Jake's arm as he leant against a wooden post. She was panting hard from the effort, yet her eyes remained fixed on his face.

"I followed you," she gasped. "I saw you going into the woods and I thought about what you'd said. I couldn't understand why you'd want to return to the place where you said your sister died."

Amelia watched him. Jake tried to relax a little. There was no evidence that the creature they'd fled from was following them; he hoped it was unable to leave the vicinity of the tree. He looked down at his torn, mud-encrusted shirt and could only marvel that Amelia hadn't deserted him.

"I owe you my life," he muttered.

"That's what sisters are for, isn't it?" Amelia said slowly.

Jake looked at her and saw tears brimming in her eyes.

"You knew?" he asked.

She shook her head. "Not until I spoke to you earlier. It made sense. Your story should have sounded crazy, but it didn't. It fitted in with what had been jumbled up inside my head and it all seemed to drop into place."

With effort, Jake pulled his body upright. "How do you feel about it?"

Amelia shrugged. "Not sure," she confessed.

Jake took a small step towards her. "Come on," he began, "we need to get out of here. I know just the person you need to talk to."

They made their way slowly up to Martha's bungalow. The need for sanctuary and a desire to get away from the woods and the monster inside it, helped Jake find the strength he required to get back.

Practically falling through the back door, Jake clung onto the edge of the kitchen work surface to stop him dropping to the floor.

Both Martha and Marion turned at their entrance. Shock filled their faces as they looked from Jake to Amelia.

"Amy?" Marion gasped.

For a moment, there was silence as they each took in the other.

"Mum?" Amelia asked, stepping around Jake.

Marion's hands flew to her mouth as a cry escaped between her lips. Her shoulders began to shake as she stepped forward, holding her arms out towards this apparition of her dead daughter.

Amelia glanced at Jake. He nodded and she moved into the embrace of their mother.

Jake felt Martha's hand sweeping his hair back from his face before he had realised she'd moved to his side.

"What happened?"

Ignoring her question, Jake held onto Martha's arms, wrapping them around his body as he rested his chin on her head. Suppressing the sobs which threatened to erupt from him, Jake buried his face into the softness of Martha's hair and closed his eyes. He forced the images of the terrible creature from his mind's eye, instead, losing himself in the warmth and security of Martha's embrace.

When Jake looked up, it was to see his mum, her face streaked with tears, smoothing Amelia's hair as she gazed into the girl's face.

The pain from his injuries had dulled, but Jake knew he must look a mess.

Martha stepped back and filled a glass with cold water. Jake took it gratefully and gulped it down.

"You went there, didn't you?" she asked, watching his shaking hands lower the glass onto the surface.

Jake nodded.

"You trying to get yourself killed?"

He remained silent as Martha's fingers began unbuttoning the buttons which remained intact on his shirt. He turned slowly as she gently peeled what remained of the garment off his body.

Gasping at the sight of the slashes across his back, Martha gingerly touched his skin around the wound.

Jake closed his eyes as though it could block out the pain which suddenly seemed to have increased. Martha's fingers were so soft and gentle in contrast to the thing which had torn through his skin as if it had been paper.

"This is bad, Jake," she sighed.

He gave a futile laugh, fully aware that his back must look horrific.

"Oh my god, Jake."

At the sound of his mum's voice, Jake opened his eyes and turned his face towards her. "I'll be fine," he said with as much gusto as he could muster.

"We need to get you to a hospital," Marion added, going to where her handbag sat and rummaging through its contents for her mobile.

"You won't get a signal up here," Jake told her.

"Where's your phone?" Marion asked Martha.

Before she could respond, Jake told his mother there wasn't one.

"We've no car," Marion stated, putting her hands in her hair. "One of us will have to go down to the pub and ring an ambulance from there for you."

"I don't need an ambulance," Jake cried. "I promise, I'll go to the hospital tomorrow but I can't leave now, not like this," he stated.

"Why not?" Marion screeched.

"Think about it!" Jake exclaimed. "What am I going to tell them happened?"

Three pairs of eyes surveyed the wields across Jake's back. The wounds were raw and angry but no longer bled.

"Who did this to you?" Marion asked, her eyes not leaving the sight of his wounds.

Jake shook his head slowly. "I can only assume it is whatever is lurking underneath that tree."

Gradually, as best he could, Jake described the creature he had seen.

"What was it?" Amelia's voice sounded frightened and lost in the brightly lit kitchen.

Jake looked at Martha. He raised his brow. "What do I say?"

"What do you remember?" Martha asked the girl.

Amelia glanced at Jake. He nodded.

"It's not so much what I remember," Amelia started, "as what Jake said helping me to make sense of the dreams which had been haunting me."

"You don't recall anything about the tree? Do you know who I am?" Martha asked

A snort of disgust from Marion was ignored.

Amelia frowned. "I always seem to end up at the tree, whenever I go into the woods; it's like I'm drawn to it," she explained. "I don't know," she said slowly, studying Martha's face. "I feel like I should know you, but I'm not sure …"

Martha and Jake looked at each other, whilst Amelia waited for a response.

Martha shook her head suddenly and, turning, disappeared into the hallway, the slamming of her bedroom door, telling Jake where she'd gone.

He stood up and grimaced. Moving to follow after Martha, he was stopped by the touch of his mum's hand on his arm.

"I'm sure we can fill you in on all this later," Marion told Amelia. "Let me sort out your brother, then we can have a proper talk."

Obediently, Amelia stepped back as Marion began running some water into the sink, holding Jake's arm to quieten him.

The lukewarm water made him wince as it trickled down his back. Amelia was ordered to go into his room and return with a clean top.

When the girl had left the room, Marion continued cleaning up her son. "We've got to leave this place as soon as possible," she told him, whispering.

"We can't just kidnap her," Jake replied, referring to Amelia. "She has a foster family she lives with now."

"I'm not leaving her here," Marion snapped. "We'll take her to the authorities in the city, they can sort it out from there, but I'm not letting either of you remain in this village for a minute longer than I have to."

Jake knew there was no point arguing with his mother when she was like this. He'd speak to her about Martha when he had to, there was no way he was leaving without her, not now.

Amelia returned holding one of his T-shirts. Jake thanked her and slipped it over his head, moving his arms stiffly. He ran his hands through his hair, specks of dirt dropping onto his clean top as he did so.

As Jake opened his mouth to speak, the whole building began to rock. Slowly at first, but rapidly increasing in intensity. Cupboard doors swung open, the glass in the windows vibrated noisily. Amelia screamed and began crying, Marion pulled the girl towards her as she leaned against the worktop, cradling her and quietly whispering into her hair.

"Where's Martha?" Jake yelled over the increasing volume of the shuddering bungalow as the sound of crashing came from various rooms.

Marion simply shook her head. "We need to get out of here," she told him.

"I'm going to get Martha," Jake replied.

"Leave her," Marion shouted. "We need to stay together."

She reached out to grab his arm but Jake ducked out of her way. "You two wait in the yard, away from the building. I'll be out in a minute," he promised, disappearing into the hallway before his mum could object.

He staggered along the corridor, holding his arms out to steady himself. "Martha?" he called as the lights suddenly went out and he was plunged into darkness.

Feeling his way along the wall, Jake stopped at her bedroom door and then pushed it open. The door slammed into the wall behind. Despite the lack of light, Jake could see the room was empty. Quickly, he hurried through the rest of the bungalow, opening doors, calling her name in rapid succession.

In the sitting room, Jake paused. One of the large windows swung open on its hinges. His mind was racing. Had she escaped when the shuddering began? Or had Martha already left her home by the time the quake started? Suddenly Jake was scared. He recalled the look on her face as she'd seen him come into the house with Amelia by his side. And she'd left them so abruptly as if she had something on her mind.

Oh no, Jake realised, the woods.

He ran back through to the kitchen as the framework of the building groaned under the increased pressure. Dust and debris rained on his head from the ceiling as he pulled the back door open and headed into the yard.

"Jake?" The sound of his mum's voice drew Jake towards the shed where he found them sheltering, her arms still around Amelia.

"She's gone, Mum. I think she's gone to the woods."

Marion grabbed her son's wrist. "Let her go, Jake," she ordered.

"No!" he cried, looking horror-struck. "I can't, I love her."

Jake watched her expression crumble, although she still clung to him.

"She killed your sister, Jake."

"No," he replied, shaking himself free of her hold. "You heard what Martha said, it wasn't her. If you insist on believing she was responsible for Amy's death then you've got to accept too that Amy killed so she could return here."

His words were like a slap. Although Marion racked her mind for a response, she knew there was nothing she could say. She was reunited with both her children and wasn't about to lose them again.

"We have to go," she told Jake. "Martha will be fine, she's strong."

Jake glared at her and slowly shook her head. "Sometimes I find it really impossible to understand you. Go if you want to, take Amelia with you, but I'm going after Martha."

Turning away, Jake felt a hand on his shoulder. He stopped and glanced back.

"You don't know where she is," Marion persisted.

"I know exactly where to find her," Jake told her and hurried along the shaking pathway.

He thought he heard his mother's voice behind him yet he didn't stop, determined now to find Martha. As Jake jogged down the field towards the woods, he realised the ground wasn't shaking as much any longer. By the time he reached the stile, everywhere was still and silent.

An almost full moon hung in the sky sending shadows darting away, in between the trees.

He grimaced in pain as he jumped down the final couple of steps of the stile, into the woods and clutched his hands to his chest. The sound of footsteps made Jake peer over the stile. He recognised Amelia coming quickly towards him, his mother followed at a short distance.

Helping Amelia, down over the stile, Jake looked at her. "You shouldn't be here," he told her as he saw his mum's hands grip the sides of the stile.

"I can help you find the way," she told him as she came to a standstill by his side.

Together they waited until Marion was next to them.

Marion glared at him. "She certainly is as stubborn as your sister used to be," she cursed.

Jake couldn't help but grin at the girl who now smiled at him. "Come on then," he whispered.

They walked in silence along the bank of the stream. Continuing past the bridge, Jake led them into the depths of the woodland, his heart beating noisily inside his bruised chest.

As they reached the vicinity of the tree, Jake turned and held his finger to his lips. Both of his companions nodded as he then continued walking.

Although it was dark, there was enough light from the moon to show their way. Jake could feel his nervousness increasing. He wanted to call out to Martha, yet was afraid of alerting the monstrosity to their approach.

Suddenly, Jake found his toes teetering on the verge of a huge hole in the ground. In his haste to avoid falling into it, he stumbled backwards, arms flapping frantically, but helpless to prevent himself dropping onto the ground.

Amelia reached down to help him up. As he got to his feet, Jake crept to his mum's side as the three of them peered down into the abyss. Their eyes met only darkness. It was a blackness darker than anything Jake had ever seen. Disbelief and confusion swept through his thoughts. Where was the tree? Where was Martha?

Minutes passed. Jake felt his mother's hand on his arm; he shook himself free. All he could think about was Martha.

"Come on," Marion said eventually as the chilliness in the air caused a sudden shiver to sweep through her body. "There's nothing you can do here now."

Reluctantly, Jake stepped back from the edge of the hole. They walked in silence back towards the distant lights of the village.

Over the next few days and weeks there was much speculation about the mysterious earthquake and the chasm which had opened in the woods, apparently as a result of the phenomenon. The woods were closed to the public, the fencing bearing huge signs explaining the dangers within.

Jake refused to go to the hospital, telling his mum the wounds would heal naturally.

Although the authorities tried arguing with Marion, the results of the blood test showed Amelia was related to her and, as the girl turned sixteen, her wish to leave her foster home and go with Jake and Marion had to be reluctantly accepted.

Whilst Jake returned to the bungalow, there was no sign of Martha. In his heart, he knew she had returned to the woods, not wishing him to risk the danger of going with her, which was why she'd crept away so furtively.

Her absence left an empty place in his heart. Jake couldn't erase her from his mind and he cried silent tears futilely for her return, hoping beyond hope that she might suddenly reappear in his life. Yet, no matter how many emails or messages Jake sent, his pleas remained unanswered.

Epilogue

It was the only thing she could do. Martha had never felt so determined, despite the wetness of the unfamiliar tears on her cheeks, she knew she was doing the right thing.

Forcing images of Jake from her mind, Martha kept putting one foot in front of the other as she hurried along the well-known path leading towards the tree.

She wasn't sure what she could do, or what to expect, but it was the only way she could think of to put an end to this nightmare and save Jake from getting hurt, or even worse, being killed. She knew he wouldn't have let her go, if she'd told him of her intentions. At the very least he would have insisted on coming with her.

Fear filled her whole being. Yet, Martha continued walking. Most of her life had been spent alone, this was nothing new to her. With Jake, she had been foolish enough to consider that happiness might finally be possible for her. Now, however, she realised how stupid she had been. In her selfishness, daring to dream of sharing a life with another human being which was filled with hope and love, she had forgotten that such things had always been out of her reach and she had been reckless to ever think that could change.

Angrily, Martha brushed bowing branches from in front of her face. Rushing along, she ignored everything around her, intent only on getting to the tree as quickly as possible, before Jake could notice she'd gone.

Facing the familiar trunk, Martha dropped to her knees in front of where she knew the hollow lay beneath it. She closed her eyes. "Please," she begged quietly, "take me back. I don't want to be here any longer. This place is cruel, only you ever gave me the love of a mother."

Pausing, Martha opened her eyes and listened. Thinking she heard a small sigh, she closed her eyes again and continued: "These people don't know how to love like you do. This world isn't worthy of our presence. Take me back with you, take me back where I belong."

Feeling the familiar hand on her own, Martha opened her eyes and saw the long, thin nails and the gnarled bony fingers.

Forcing away the disgust rising in her throat, Martha tried to clear her mind. With a final look behind her, she pushed her way down, below the trunk and into the hollow. Glad of the darkness which greeted her, Martha felt a cloak wrap around her shoulders as she was pulled further into the space below the tree.

"Let's go," she whispered. "We don't need them. I promise, I'll stay with you. I'll never ask to leave you again."

Martha screwed her eyes up tightly as the ground began to shake around her. The touch of a kiss on her cheek sent a shudder through her body but she kept her eyes firmly closed, ignoring the moistness of the tears against her eye lashes.

Fighting against the desire to call out Jake's name, Martha bit her lip as she felt herself falling into the old, familiar place of oblivion which welcomed her home, back into its embrace.

THE END

Made in the USA
Columbia, SC
18 September 2017